Facing North

Tales from Bathsheba

Edison T Williams

TO
RON
ENJOY!

Edison

This book is a work of fiction. The events, characters, names and incidents described are products of the author's imagination. Any resemblance to persons alive or dead is coincidental.

Published by Edison T. Williams
Old Mill House
Clermont, St. James
Barbados BB23024

ISBN: 978–976–8233–66–0 (E-Book)
ISBN: 978–976–8233–68–4 (paperback)
ISBN: 978–976–8233–69–1 (hard cover)
Website: www.storiesfrombarbados.com

ISBN: 9-7682-3368-0
ISBN-13: 9789768233684

Dedicated to Richard Stanton Cox, born 18th December 1970

Contents

Acknowledgements

I consider myself fortunate to live in a country that offers its citizens opportunities to be taught by such outstanding teachers and writers. I wish to thank my writing teachers–Robert Edison Sandiford at Barbados Community College and Professor George Lamming at the University of the West Indies, Cave Hill. Apologies are due to them for my boldness in bringing up my association with them, for I am aware that a poor student may be considered a poor advertisement of the quality of instruction. My greatest wish will be fulfilled only when my efforts receive acknowledgement deserving of their association.

I also wish to thank every teacher who taught me throughout my school years both at St. Silas and Harrison College, but in particular Mr. Johnson who encouraged my interest in writing at HC. He thought his job was to teach us how to think. My school disagreed and sent him back whence he came. I never forgot him.

Heartfelt thanks go out to my wife, Margaret, my first reader and chief supporter; my son Alex, and daughter, Zahra, for their special assistance; sister and brothers, Pauline, James, CQ, and brother-in-law Laurie for their encouragement; my late parents, Clyde and Ena, my first teachers, who taught me that there are no limits; and Bathsheba, for inspiring me.

The author has had a professional career as a hotelier and restaurateur. He took up writing short stories as part of his retirement activities.
He has won several awards for his writing in Barbados' National Independence Festival of Creative Arts.
His work has appeared on ArtsEtcbarbados.com.

Author's Note

Bathsheba, even on a good map, is but a dash on the side of this dot of an island called Barbados. It lies on its eastern, or Atlantic, coast between Foster Hall and Cattlewash and below Hackleton's Cliff. It is a quiet seaside village of fishermen, farmers and other folk. It is also a long-time vacation spot for locals and a handful of visitors. But those visitors who stay in Bathsheba are atypical of the usual Barbados holiday-maker. Some are seekers of a different experience in what for them is the *real Barbados*. Others are seekers of solace, seclusion, even concealment.

Bathsheba is a place of natural beauty and is an obligatory stop for myriad visitors touring the island. They drive through in buses, taxis and hired cars, pointing their cameras at what can only seem, to them, like a sleepy seaside village. The uniqueness of this place, fortunately, lost to the multitude.

Bathsheba's salty sea air is thought to have recuperative powers and Bathsheba itself was once known as a place for convalescence. It is also considered by some to be a spiritual place. Some Barbadians stand at the shoreline and gaze directly out to sea believing that they are looking eastward, and connecting to Mother Africa. But Bathsheba is positioned on the north-facing section of a long curved bay, so they are in fact facing north towards Europe. This "lie of the land, this trick of nature," as a character in one of the stories describes it, is perhaps a metaphor for this nation and has inspired the title of the collection.

These fictional stories are about the drama of life in a small community. They also deal with the way in which the villagers' lives can from time to time be impacted by its transient residents.

Although Barbadian, I am not a Bathsheban. I chose to set these tales in Bathsheba as a token of my affection for the place and its people.

Edison T. Williams

The Price of Fish

Bashaow! Alfred sprang upright at the sound of the second crash of the waves. Half awake when he heard the first bashaow of water pounding sand and rocks, he thought he had been dreaming. It was around four thirty in the morning, not yet light. He swung out of bed, walked over to the chair next to the bedroom door and picked up the pair of swimming trunks, shorts and tee-shirt he had left there the night before.

Isalene watched him dress and followed him to the back door of their blue and cream chattel-house. *Bashaow*, another wave crashed. She stood behind him at the door, threw her arms around his chest, a hand over his heart, and held on briefly. "Go good," she said. "It don't sound good," he replied. He heard the door close behind him. He thought she would go back to bed but knew she wouldn't go back to sleep.

Alfred walked briskly down the hill, hoping it was not as bad as it sounded. He turned right into Tent Bay and made out a figure ahead also moving quickly. As he drew closer he recognized the bow-legged gait and leftward list of Alson Broomes. Alfred caught up with him as they reached the Sea-U Guest House. "Mornin', Pa Broomes. Where this weather come from?" *Bashaow*, another wave crashed followed this time by the splintering of wood.

"Oh, God," boomed Alson, peering in the direction of the sound even though it was too dark to see anything, "a boat gone." His loud voice was something of a surprise; He was no taller than five-foot-six. Perhaps it was a habit developed from having constantly to compete with the noise of a fishing boat motor against the background of the ocean.

They picked up pace. "We got to get the boats out," said Alfred. They took the shortcut through the grounds of the old Atlantis Hotel and down the broken steps to what was once the bed of the old train track, now a natural breakwater.

Wind whistled through their clothes. Electric power lines whined. Dogs barked. Lights came on in the houses around the bay.

Where had this weather come from? Were the weathermen caught napping again? There were nine boats in the water last night. How many would survive this?

"You got you phone?" asked the old man.

"No," answered Alfred, patting pockets with both hands.

Groggy and Seaman arrived from the other end of the bay, breathing heavily. Light from a pair of headlamps curved through the darkness as a vehicle made its way down the hill and took the sharp left around the bend at the eastern entrance to Tent Bay. The driver positioned the pick-up facing the moored boats. The handbrake made a raking sound, the diesel motor kept running and the head lights stayed on. The men could see pieces of wood that had once been a boat, now bobbing flotsam. One piece, painted bright yellow, bore the number O 542 in large black lettering. Day boats carried a number on the roof of the cabin for easy identification in a search-and-rescue situation. O 542 was the number of Abraham Bend's boat. Nature's power had found a weak link, snapped the boat from its mooring and smashed it against the nearby rocks. "High wind know where old house live," his grandmother used to say. The other eight fishing boats were still there riding the swells, dancing with the flows until their ties to the anchored buoys pulled them back sharply, just like a strong parent pulling a child away from danger.

The driver got out of the pick-up, phone in hand. "Anybody call the tractor man?"

"I left my phone home, I was just going up to the hotel to make a call," said Alson.

"By the time he get here it might be too late," said Alfred.

More men and a woman arrived. They grumbled because there was no longer a tractor garaged right there in Tent Bay. It had been deemed an underuse of a resource and redeployed, called on only when needed. This was one of those times but the tractor man didn't answer his phone. The driver of the pick-up suggested a call to the Member of Parliament. Someone called out his home number, another person called out his mobile phone number. "He coming," said the driver, "one of the neighbours call he already." That wouldn't happen in a big country Alfred said to himself.

They paced up and down. Some on the bed of the old train tracks, some down on the rocky ramp leading into the sea. Ideas were tossed around. Dawn approached.

The MP arrived, quickly, eager to help. "I can't raise Mr. Roach," he told the fishermen. "I called the Minister of Works. He could get a tractor here in an hour and a half." There was a chorus of "Too long, man too long." The MP paced up and down with phone to ear, exasperation on his face.

The boats continued to strain at their moorings, rising with each wave and crashing down after the wave had passed. How long could the moorings hold was the question on everyone's mind?

More fishermen and villagers arrived.

"We have to take the boats out to the deep," said Alfred, sounding eager to get on with it. Even though he had inherited his, he, like every other fisherman, knew the value of his boat. But uppermost in his mind was the promise he had made to his late father.

. He knew that the life-jackets were in the boats and they would have to swim the more than two hundred meters against the raging tide, unaided. That rage had destroyed the concrete jetty built there some years ago. The older fishermen had deemed it a waste of money from conception and predicted its demise. They had been ignored by planners with degrees and contractors who, they thought, should have known better. But these hardy men who made a living in these waters, men who took their small day boats more than twenty miles off shore on a regular basis, they knew this sea. They had seen its power time and time again. They also had confidence in their boats which they had built themselves right there in Tent Bay, outside of the new fish market. Alfred was worried about Alson. More worried about his age than his appearance. The old man was seventy if he was a day, but you wouldn't guess it by looking at those sinewy shoulders and arms. And he was the one who had done this most, the one who had braved many seas like this, the one who had told the stories to the younger fishermen.

Dawn was breaking. The sun, obscured by dark clouds, cast a dim glow over the ocean. The truck driver turned off his engine and lights.

Alson addressed the fishermen. "You got to aim straight at the wave, full throttle, one at a time. Wait for the man in front you to go clear." He talked about the swim. "Alferd, you go first."

Why had he been chosen? Was it because he was the youngest, or perhaps because Alson had been his father's best friend and wanted him in front where he could see him? And why did Alson always call him Alferd? Alfred walked down the ramp and into the surf.

He thought of his surfing buddies who would be out with their boards at the other end of Bathsheba. He would have preferred to be with them now, but he had to be here. He stood there, a broad shouldered, full-chested young man, yet but a small creature in front of this infinite and angry ocean churning its way towards him.

"I can do this, I can do this." He repeated to himself, shaking his fingers loosely at his side. He waited for a wave to recede and followed it. "I wish I was surfing," he said to himself as he dived into the water.

Maude Griffith, old fish seller, dressed as usual in a long dress and head tie, started to pray aloud. "Calm these waters, Lord. Calm these waters. I beseech you, I command you to protect these men."

Alfred remembered the old man's words. "You got to go under the big waves." He thought that one day he might have to be the one giving the same advice and shuddered at the thought. He didn't know if he could ask others to do what he was about to do. He was a mechanic not really a fisherman. He fixed motor car and boat engines. But his father told him time and again, "When things hard on land, there will always be fish in the sea. Never give up this boat."

He swam hard with the ebbs, head just out of the water and pivoting with each stroke, breathing left, breathing right and keeping an eye on the boats. He took a deep breath as a big wave approached and dived under. The water tugged at his body, pulling him back. He was treading water, treading water, lungs beginning to strain, then it released him, letting him swim again. He surfaced, his mouth flew open. Air, sweet as fresh cane juice, filled his lungs. He thought of his dead father, Cleophus. Old Cleophus was there with him. He felt safe. He looked around and saw that he was off course; the boats were over to his left now. He changed direction and charged ahead. He finally reached the *Lady Janet*. She was the third *Lady Janet* in his family but there was no number after her name to indicate succession. Old Cleophus didn't like that. He had built them all, the first one out of mahogany brought down by hurricane Janet in 1955. Alfred grabbed the tyre hanging by a rope from the side of the boat. He hung on, gasping like a fish just hauled on board. Isalene flashed across his mind. She would be up and about finding things to do, maybe making breakfast for their two-year-old son if he was up, busily trying to ignore the distant, incessant roar of the sea only to be reminded each time she heard *bashaow*.

He pulled himself up over the blue-painted side. He thought he heard Sister Griffith yell, "Amen, thank you, Lord." He flopped in the bottom of the boat, listened to the rapid beating of his heart and watched his stomach rise and fall. "Let that damn hotel manager tell me how much I should charge for my fish next time."

Alfred got to his feet swaying with each pitch of the boat. He held on to the side and looked for the men who had followed him into the water. He started to count heads in the water. He spotted Groggy, then Seaman, George Bishop, Brock, Dalton Greene and back of the pack, Alson and Tallman together. Alson had drifted wide, but Tallman the strongest swimmer in the group, was right there with him; these were men risking their lives to save their living, men for whom heroics are a part of normal life. One by one they reached the boats, watched by an entranced crowd on the shore and fascinated hotel guests on their balconies.

The *Lady Janet's* engine clattered and roared. The sound of the 100-horse power motor reverberated across the bay against the roar of the ocean, challenging it, telling it, "I will defeat you today." Alfred waited for the passage of the next wave before he detached from his mooring.

He steered the *Lady Janet* toward the channel, the break in the reef that permitted safe entry to and exit from the bay. He aimed the tapered bow at the oncoming wave and gave the *Lady Janet* the full throttle. The boat lifted as it hit the wave, and with its bottom completely clear of the water, seemed to fly. "Yeahhhh," yelled Alfred. But his cry of exultation was drowned out by the high-pitched whirring of the boat's propeller spinning in air. That shrill sound remained etched in his memory of the day's events.

The spectacle produced gasps on the shore. Cameras clicked on hotel balconies. Sister Griffith raised her hands and shouted, "Behold the power of the Lord, he doth raise the boat above the raging waters."

The *Lady Janet* hit the water and engine barking, moved on to meet the next wave. She rose and fell again and moved beyond the reef into open water.

One after the other the engines roared, the boats headed for the channel. Each boat performed the same routine until the eighth and last boat made it out. The taut faces they left on the shore would be relaxed now. They would be joking and laughing to hide their nervousness and Sister Griffith would be thanking the Lord for their safety. The MP would be talking to Abraham Bend trying to see what help he might need to get a boat back in the water. The crowd would stay there until the boats were completely out of sight

The convoy of boats, with Alfred at its head, bobbed and weaved its way through the heaving water. They rounded the northern tip of the island and headed down the west coast to safety.

Facing North

Peter Devonish had just settled into his chair on the back terrace of his Chancery Lane home, drink in hand, when the telephone rang from somewhere inside the house. "Where is the damn phone, Monica?"

"It's just where you left it, dear," responded his wife from her lounge chair without looking up from the novel she was reading.

Peter set down his drink, tumbled out of his seat and hurried indoors to find the telephone before the call went to voice mail. The portable phone was on the granite counter top between the fridge and the sink, just where he left it when he fetched the ice for his rum and water. He was about to speak but the caller immediately addressed him. He recognized the voice right away.

"Yes, Brad."

Peter ambled back to the terrace, phone to ear, sank his six-foot frame into his chair and picked up his drink with his free hand.

As soon as the telephone call ended Monica asked, "Who was that?" and closed her book, an indication to Peter that she was expecting more than a name for an answer. After twenty years of marriage he understood when she wanted details.

"It was Brad Fielder down at the house in Bathsheba. He wants to talk to me about a personal matter. He was a bit vague but it doesn't sound like anything too serious."

Monica took a sip of her white wine and said, "Hmm. I hope that daughter of his hasn't gotten herself in any trouble with one of those beach boys."

"Don't be silly. Kathy is only fourteen." Facing North

"Yeah, fourteen going on twenty-four," Monica replied. "They have been staying in Bathsheba for the last five years and know all kinds of people down there. She and her brother are very friendly with those surfer boys, you know."

"Why don't we just wait to find out whatever the problem is? What's for dinner?

"It's too early to eat, dear, and why are you trying to change the subject?"

"Why do you always answer a question with a question?"

"Do I really?" Monica smirked, exposing those dimples Peter admired. She picked up her book and started to read again. Peter just looked at her without replying. She was a handsome woman, tall with smooth dark-chocolate skin, big, knowing eyes that sparkled, and unfussy, close-cropped hair.

Peter took another sip of his drink. He thought about Brad Fielder. He remembered the first time he heard the man's voice. It must have been six years ago. It had roused Peter out of a Sunday afternoon nap. He was still groggy when he picked up the phone but the voice at the other end fully woke him up. It was deep and unmistakably American, from the south. It was the voice of a big man.

"Hello, you must be Peter." The voice didn't pause for an answer but just continued speaking slowly and deliberately. "I am calling about the green bungalow with the wooden deck in Bathsheba. I would like to rent it, next year, for two weeks in February—if you have availability, that is. I was in Bathsheba earlier today with my family. We're from Chicago. We fell in love with the area and we met your caretaker, Rabbit, on the beach. He told us about the villa and showed us around. The price is just right. I can't believe the difference in price from the west coast. We'll make a deposit before we leave next Tuesday. Just tell me how I can do that." Brad Fielder spoke as if he had rehearsed his lines.

Part of the uniqueness of Bathsheba was the type of visitor it attracted. Bathsheba renters were not typical of the Barbadian visitor. They were not content to lie on the beach or to go on organised tours. They were seekers of a Barbados they believed to be the *Real Barbados*. Bathsheba was an un-gated community where holiday accommodation was intermixed with local housing and renters could become a part of the local community.

Brad Fielder and his family became annual tenants of Peter's, or more truthfully of Monica's as the beach house was hers, an inheritance from her grandfather, Charles Corbin the attorney. Monica was his only granddaughter and he had adored her.

She and Peter renovated the house nine years ago and put it on the international rental market. While the interior was modern, they retained its original West Indian colonial styling on the exterior, sash windows with hoods and jalousie shutters. They incorporated the old small veranda into the living room and added a new veranda which ran the length of the front of the house. It was all now very attractive and drew admiring glances from everyone.

Rabbit came with the house. A Bathsheba man all his life, he rarely left the village. An energetic slightly built man who took short brisk steps as he went about his tasks. He never missed a day's work and during his early morning visits kept the property tidy. He was a handyman and worked for other properties as well but had a special relationship with Monica's grandfather.

"Mr. Corbin was a very nice man. I looked after him and I am going to look after you," he told Monica. His nickname had nothing to do with furry little animals but rather with an incident at Sunday school when he was a boy and had misread the word rabbi while reading to the class, causing an eruption of laughter and giving him a second monicker.

Casa de Carlos (Monica retained the name in honour of her grandfather) had built up a good repeat clientele which now included the Fielders: Brad, an ex-college football coach turned successful insurance executive, and his wife, Cindy, an ex-schoolteacher. Peter and his wife had developed a friendship with them and always met up for lunch or dinner with their family while they were in Barbados.

∝∝

Peter guided his SUV through the countryside in the direction of Bathsheba. As he crested Horse Hill, he caught that first glimpse of one of nature's great gifts to Barbados. Off to his left he could see the rolling hills of the east coast, their feet covered in golden sands and toes bathed in the churning surf. For him this was just a teaser, to titillate his appetite for the main course, Bathsheba. Peter never tired of its magnificent scenery. As usual he approached from the Community Centre end. From there, he could see to his left the mushroom rocks like giant misshaped heads jutting out of the sand or the shallow end of the Atlantic Ocean. Further left, steep hills with houses sprinkled among the trees. Tall coconut trees punctuated the panorama like giant bushy-topped exclamation marks.

Peter followed the winding road along the coast until he came to Pops' rum-shop. He pulled the SUV off the road onto a little grassy area in front of Pops'. He saw Brad standing next to an umbrella with a Banks beer in his hand. He was a burly figure of a man, six-foot-three -or-four. His reddish brown hair, highlighted in the dying embers of the waning sun, seemed redder than brown.

He was a little paunchy but most men would hesitate before tackling him, even though he was now in his mid fifties.

Brad was in conversation with Tony Holford, better known as Three Schools in Bathsheba. He was an old school friend of Peter's. Tony was a regular at Pops and it was the only place that Peter ever saw him. They had gone their different ways after school.

"What's happening, Holie?"

"All the happenings with you, Devilish," replied Tony with a wide grin, exposing cigarette-stained teeth in the middle of his gray-flecked goatee.

"Hi, Brad."

"Hey, Peter, good to see you."

Peter shook hands with the two men.

"Let me say hello to Pops," said Peter as he headed inside and up to the bar.

"I'll have a Mount Gay Extra Old and water, Pops," said Peter looking around at the advertising posters with nearly nude girls on the wall. "How is Eldica?"

"Dica good, man. You know, she got me to look after she, so she got to be good." Pops threw back his round bald head and laughed. His entire face lit up, gold teeth flashed. Typical Pops. Everything was always right with his world, it seemed to Peter.

"Say hello to her for me."

Drink in hand, Peter headed back outside to where he had left Brad and Tony. The three men headed to the lone umbrella-covered picnic table on the outside of the bar.

"Peter, I was saying to Tony that this is the first time I have seen him in quite a while. I don't think we saw him at all last year."

Peter nodded.

Brad recalled the story of the Fielders' first encounter with Tony.

Cindy had roused the family early their first morning in Bathsheba and taken them down to the beach to watch the sunrise. They were sitting on the sand looking out to sea when this man passed behind them and said, "If you keep facing north, you'll never see the sunrise."

Cindy called after him for an explanation.

"Turn 90 degrees to your right and wait a few minutes," he said and continued on his morning walk. They were a little confused, but they turned to the right and watched as the tip of the orange ball burst out of the horizon and kept on rising. As the earth dipped, the sun added new colour to the ocean, a mix of greens and blues, and the pre-dawn gray disappeared. "Damn it. I should have brought my paints and brushes," shouted Cindy, shaking her fists. They were still there when Tony returned and Brad stopped him to ask more questions.

Tony told him that many Barbadians made the same mistake, believing that they were looking east to Africa when in fact they were looking north to Europe. "You see, Bathsheba is positioned on the north-facing section of this long curved bay." He stretched both arms out as he explained. "So this lie of the land, this trick of nature could be a metaphor for this nation of Afro-Saxons who face Europe and think of Africa."

"You actually called us Afro-Saxons," Peter said. Tony chuckled.

"I'll leave you to think about that," he said and headed into the bar.

"You know he reminds me a bit of Cindy's Dad who used to be a hippy in college but later got rid of his long hair and beard. Some of his friends say his beliefs as well."

Brad paused and then continued, "Thanks for coming to see me, my friend. I need a bit of advice and you are the best person I know in Barbados to advise me. This is our fifth year staying in Bathsheba and we love this place, from the very first time we saw it. We were staying on the west coast and took an island tour with a taxi when we came down that hill and saw this stunning piece of landscape. It just took our breath away. Cindy was ecstatic; she wrote a poem about that first sight of Bathsheba. From the next year this was our holiday home. I just spend one week because I have to get back home to Chicago to take care of business but Cindy and the kids stay for the full two weeks, her parents join them for the second week, as you know. And man I have to admit that arrangement gives me a bit of breathing space. And we so love the people here. We always take good care of Rabbit, and Shirley, who is a gem of a cook by the way." His voice dropped to what was a whisper for Brad. "Now here is the problem. You know Sam Coochie the surfer?"

It sounded more like a statement than a question but Peter nodded and said, "I think you mean Sam Rice."

"Tall, good-looking feller, he is also something of a painter. In fact Cindy always buys one of his paintings to take home each year. She thinks he's got talent." Brad took a cigarette from the pack on the table and lit up. "Sam taught Kathy and Brad Junior to surf. Brad is now a junior surfing champion back in the

US. He went out to California to compete, which is why he is not here this year. He is staying with Cindy's sister. Two years ago Sam approached Cindy and me for a loan to help with replacing a fishing boat owned by him and his brother. It had been damaged in the storm the year before. The boat had not been insured and he wanted to replace it."

Peter interrupted. "Sam is no fisherman, you know. Sam's brother is the real fisherman. Sam only goes fishing occasionally. He spends a lot of his time surfing and painting Bathsheba scenes to sell to tourists."

"Well, I lent him five thousand dollars, which is ten thousand in Bajan money, to help get a new boat, but he has never paid me back one cent. Now if I was back in Chicago I would know just how to deal with this, but I thought I should ask your advice on how I should handle things here."

Peter stroked his chin and said, "Tell me something. Did you get Sam to sign any sort of an agreement?"

"No, we shook hands on it."

"You shook hands on it? Would you do that back in Chicago?"

"No! But I would back in Knox City, the little Texas town where I grew up. Cindy did tell me at the time to have him sign something but I decided against it because he seemed like such a nice guy. She is a California girl. Not as trusting as us Texans."

"Does he acknowledge the debt?"

"Well, we are about to find out. What should I do?"

"Providing he acknowledges the debt, you should take Cindy's advice and get him to sign an agreement setting out a repayment schedule. I can ask Monica to draw up the agreement for you."

"You will ask her? Good man." Brad took a long puff on his cigarette. "Of course, she should bill me for her fees. Your glass is empty. Let me get you another drink."

"No, thanks, I am going to head back to Chancery Lane but I will get Monica to call you."

"Thank you, my friend."

They stood to say their goodbyes. "I don't see a car," said Peter. "Shall I give you a lift back to the house?"

"I'll walk. I need the exercise and you forget that Cindy does the driving here. I don't like driving on the wrong side of the road. So she gets to do all the running around, while I get to relax," Brad said with a laugh.

"Take care, then, and say hello to Cindy and the Kathy. We'll see you on Saturday."

Brad set off back to *Casa De Carlos* with a bit of a totter, thought Peter, as he entered the rum-shop to settle up with Pops. Things were picking up in the bar now as some youngsters had come in to watch English football on a Spanish Channel on Pops' satellite TV. The TV had been the only addition to Pops' shop in twenty years.

Peter wanted to talk to Pops, who was a storehouse of local current affairs, but the shop was too busy. He said goodbye to Pops and turned to see Tony in the corner, drink in hand and watching a game of draughts. It was draughts that gave Tony the nickname *Three Schools*. Tony was the lone university graduate among the regulars. One day he was beaten at draughts by an old man who declared, "I only went to one school but I beat a three-school man," much to the amusement of the onlookers. He walked over to say goodbye to Tony and ended up chatting for about fifteen minutes then went on his way.

৵৵

In Chancery Lane that evening, over dinner, Peter discussed with Monica his earlier meeting with Brad. "It should not be too difficult a matter. Once the debt is acknowledged in writing, the agreement could be enforced. Brad could take a lien on the boat," said Monica, "but it could get complicated if Sam denies ever receiving the money. I can draw up the agreement tomorrow if I get the details. I'll call Brad after dinner."

"I saw Tony Holford at Pops' bar."

"What is he up to these days?"

"He is still working in the Ministry of Finance and passing his evenings at Pops' playing dominoes and draughts with the boys and handing out his pearls of wisdom. He is an atheist now, apparently."

"Gosh, the gifted often don't know who to thank for their talents."

"Oh, come on, Monica, who should the un-gifted thank for their lack of talent?"

"You are looking for an argument, Devonish, but not tonight. I am going to call Brad."

৵৵

Brad and Cindy sat on the deck at the back of the house. They had retired there after dinner to relax with a couple of drinks, look at the stars and listen to the choir of tree frogs croak their way through their repertoire. Their daughter had gone to bed.

"Peter doesn't seem to think that it will be too big a problem," said Brad.

"But he is not the lawyer, Monica is. Why didn't you speak to her in the first place? No, you had to speak to the man."

Brad ignored the question. "Tell me something, do you think we should be concerned about how fond Kathy and Sam seem to be of each other?"

"Not really. Your daughter is a naturally friendly person but she is also a very sensible girl."

"But she *is* very impressionable."

"Not so impressionable that she would give away five thousand dollars without an agreement." Cindy paused then added, "I told you so two years ago, Brad, but you never listen to me, do you?"

"OK, knock it off. You forget it was your idea to lend him the money in the first place? Let's go to bed."

"It is just that we have so much. You know five thousand dollars is not an awful lot of money to us."

"Yeah, but that doesn't mean that we can just toss it away. We worked too hard for it."

Brad got up and stretched, his hands reaching into the leaves of the almond tree which shaded the deck during the day.

The telephone rang as they were making their way back into the house. Brad answered. It was Monica.

"Sorry to hear about Sam. You are supposed to be here to relax and have fun, not deal with problems. Now, it would be very easy for me to draw up an agreement, I just need a few details."

Brad answered Monica's questions. His secretary had sent the money via Western Union. Sam lived up the hill in St. Elizabeth Village. The repayments could be made directly to Monica, who could apply them to future rent. He didn't want the repayment schedule to be too onerous. He accepted Monica's suggestion on this. There were other questions Brad answered and Monica said she could get the agreement down to him after lunch the following day.

"Kathy is going surfing in the morning. She will see Sam. I will have her ask him to come up to the house," said Brad.

❦❧

The agreement arrived about 2 o'clock by motorcycle courier. Later that afternoon Sam Rice came up to *Casa de Carlos*. Sam was about five-foot, eleven inches with a wiry build, a lean handsome face and a stud in each earlobe. His head was shaved bald.

"You wanted to see me, Mr. Fielder?"

They sat on the veranda and Brad said, "It's about the money we loaned you."

Sam responded instantly, "You don't have to worry, Mr. Fielder, Sam going to pay you back every penny."

"Well, we would appreciate you signing something acknowledging the debt and agreeing to a repayment schedule."

"That is no problem, man. I was planning to bring you some money before you leave, anyway. You don't have to worry. We had to pay back some other debts after we get the boat back in the water, but I getting back on my feet now. So you don't have to worry, Mr. Fielder."

"All right, Sam. Come inside and have a look at the agreement."

They moved to the dining room and sat at the table. Sam's cell phone rang; he glanced at the number calling and turned off the phone. He proceeded to read the agreement. Brad passed him a pen and he affixed his signature with a flourish. Brad also signed on the dotted line below Sam.

The following morning Brad asked Rabbit to witness their signatures. He showed him only the area where the signatures were affixed. Rabbit slowly signed his full name, Elroy DaCosta Gaskin.

ॐ ॐ

Two days later, Friday, when Kathy returned from the beach, she informed her parents that Sam would be coming to see them about four o'clock that evening. Sam showed up on time and just as Shirley was leaving.

"Hey, Sam, you got something for me?" asked Shirley with a giggle, pointing to the brown briefcase in Sam's hand.

"I ain't got nothing for you, Shirley Holder, but you can tell Shonia I say hello."

"I ain't carrying no message to my daughter for the likes of you. Shonia would never talk to you again, Sam Coochie."

"Who you callin' Sam Coochie? I am *Mr. Rice* to you, please," snarled Sam.

"Mr. Rice? You must be mean Mr. Mice, you old rat. I don't know why you don't stop trying to fool young girls. I done tell Mr. Brad to watch out for you, you know." Shirley was interrupted by the approaching sound of the Fielders as they entered the veranda. She cut her eyes at Sam, pushed up her mouth and left.

"Good evening, Mr. Fielder, Mistress Fielder. Can we go inside? I would prefer not to talk on the gallery."

"Sure," said Brad, leading the way and ushering Sam to a seat at the dining table.   Brad and Sam sat across from each other and Cindy sat at the head of the table.

"How can we help you?" asked Brad.

Sam placed his briefcase on the table and proceeded to open it. He said, "I come to pay you back."

Brad and Cindy looked at each other, open mouthed, and then back to Sam. He took a brown paper bag out of the briefcase. He stuck his hand inside and pulled out a wad of assorted bank notes. He placed it in front of Brad.

"You can check it, it all there," Sam said. There was a confidence bordering on cockiness about Sam that evening, Brad would later comment to Cindy. "I'd never seen that in him before."

Silence in the room. Brad Fielder, who never seemed lost for words and rarely paused between his words, was speechless. He pulled out his pack of cigarettes, lit one and inhaled deeply.

"Sam, I have to ask you this. Where did you get this money? You haven't done anything illegal, have you?" asked Cindy, scepticism etched on her face and in her tone of voice.

Sam recoiled and raised his voice slightly. "I am a strictly legal man, Cindy …Miss Fielder."

"I need a drink. Anybody else?" Brad asked.

"I will take a beer," said Sam with a smile.

"Nothing for me," said Cindy.

As Brad got up from the table, there was a slight scuffling of feet from the living room. He went in the direction of the noise just in time to catch a glimpse of Kathy going onto the veranda. Brad stood where he was for a few seconds then turned around and went to the kitchen, where he filled a glass with ice and some of Shirley's rum punch. "Just what I need," he said to himself. He swigged half the glass of rum punch and refilled the glass. He took a beer out of the fridge and returned to the dining room.

"Look, I had some of this money save and was going to surprise you before you leave," Sam was saying to Cindy. "After you speak to me I went and speak to Three Schools. He advise me to try and pay you back one time, otherwise I could end up in court or even go to jail."

Brad cut him off. "We weren't trying to take you to court; it was just a case of safeguarding our interest. You understand."

"Well, Schools tell me to go all out to pay you back. He say he could help with some. He is a man with a Government job and me and he, we get on real good. He say he would also have a word with Pops for me. I didn't want anybody else to know 'bout the situation. But I say, "All right." Pops is a decent man, he and my mother used to talk. Between me, my brother, Three Schools and Pops, we put it together. So we square now?"

"Just let me count it out," said Brad, proceeding to leaf through the wad of notes. There was mostly Barbadian currency but also US dollars, a few Euros, Canadian dollars and British pounds.

"I take any currency that the bank will take. I learn that from Pops," explained Sam.

Brad did some mental calculations and said, "I'll have to check the exchange rates but it looks like it could be about right."

"It more than right, Schools check it for me. Can we tear up the paper that I sign, now?"

"I think so… I don't see why not," said Brad.

"Hold on a minute," said Cindy putting up a hand. We should *not* tear up the agreement. We simply need to write you a receipt marked paid in full. I believe that would be the correct procedure in the circumstances."

"I think you are right," Brad said. "Sam, let me write up a receipt right away." Brad took another swig of Shirley's rum punch, shuffled the notes together and took them with him to his and Cindy's bedroom. He reached for a notepad and composed a receipt. He placed the paper bag with the money in the drawer of his bedside table, returned to the dining room and handed the receipt to Sam.

Sam rose to leave. "I going to catch the five o'clock bus. I sleeping down in town by my grandmother tonight."

Brad and Cindy walked him to the door and as he headed off to the bus stop they turned and looked at each other. Without saying a word they headed back indoors, pausing in the living room.

"Do you believe him about where he got the money?" said Brad.

"We have no choice but to believe him. We accepted the payment in good faith," said Cindy.

"We should give Peter and Monica the good news," said Brad

"Are you forgetting that we are meeting them for lunch tomorrow? Gosh, you are becoming so forgetful, Brad." Cindy let out a deep sigh and headed for the kitchen. "I am going to fix supper. Aren't you hungry?"

৵৽

Cindy awoke around 5.30 the next morning. Brad was still snoring. She lay there until he stirred. He slowly woke and his attention was drawn to the drape in front of the glass sliding door. It moved, blown by the wind. It did it again and Cindy suddenly said, "Brad Fielder! We've got ten thousand dollars in our room and you go and leave the sliding door open. It's a good thing we aren't back in Chicago."

"What are you talking about? Not me. I thought I saw you close it last night"

Cindy got out of bed and made her way to the sliding door. She pulled back the drape. "Are you sure you didn't open this door?"

Fully awake now, Brad turned and opened the drawer of the bedside table. "Oh, my God. The money is gone, Cindy. Did you move it?"

"Why would I do that?"

"Well, it's not here. It's gone."

"Jesus Christ! The whole ten thousand? You mean someone came in here and took it while we were asleep? Jesus Christ!"

There was a knock at the door. Kathy called out. "Mom, Dad, what's going on?"

Brad rushed to the door and opened it. He hauled Kathy in by one arm. "Did you come into our room last night?"

"No—I didn't. Ow! You're hurting me. What is going on?"

"Sam paid us the money he owed us yesterday and now it's gone. Someone came in while we were asleep and took it," said her mother.

"And Dad thinks I took it?"

"Oh, no, sweetheart, I was only asking if -"

"If what, Dad? If what? Did I steal from my own parents? I can't believe you would think that I would do such a thing." Kathy started to cry.

"Oh, no, sweetheart." Brad put his arm around her and hugged her closely.

"Brad, we need to call Monica and Peter. Kathy, sweetheart, please go and have some breakfast."

Cindy sat on the bed, placed her elbows on her knees, bent forward and nestled her face in her palms.

Brad went to the telephone and dialled.

"Is that you, Peter?" he asked before the person who picked up could speak.

"No, it's Monica. Brad, is something wrong?"

"I am afraid so. We've been robbed."

"Robbed?"

"Sam Coochie came yesterday evening and paid us the ten thousand dollars he owed us. Someone broke in last night and stole it. All of it."

"That's unbelievable …. Who knew it was in the house?"

"Well, at least Sam plus Three Schools and Pops and Sam's brother."

"And probably the rest of Bathsheba. That's too many people to keep a secret. Have you called the police?"

"Do you think that's necessary?"

"Brad, what would you do if your home in Chicago was burgled?"

"I would call the police for sure."

"I will also report the matter to our insurers. They will need that police report. But I am not sure what position the insurance will take because of the amount of cash. They don't like homeowners keeping large sums at home."

Cindy did not want to call the police, either. She was concerned that there would be questions about the source of Sam's funds and that it could be a problem for him. But Brad insisted. "You don't pay a lawyer to take your own advice," he said.

The police arrived at *Casa de Carlos* at around 8:30. At 8:37 the telephone rang. Cindy answered. It was Shirley.

"Mistress, I hear de police down there. Wha' happen?"

"Someone broke in and stole some money while we were asleep."

"Hav'is mercy, Lord, come for your world. You all is decent people. You mean they couldn't find nobody else to rob? Excuse me for asking, but why you all keep money in the house like that?"

"It was some money that Sam paid us back yesterday."

"Who Sam? Sam Coochie? De police could go straight to he house. He is no good, Miss Cindy. I don't like to see he round dat house, you know. I try to warn you bout he every long time since. He is no blasted good. Excuse me. Look, I comin' down there right now."

"It's your off day, Shirley. And you are wrong about Sam. He wasn't even in Bathsheba last night. He went to his grandmother's in town."

"He went to he grandmother? Dat is bare tricks. You ain't know who you dealing with. As soon as my husband come back, I comin' down there."

Cindy hung up then went to the living room window. A small group had gathered on the other side of the road. Rabbit was in the middle of the group. He kept shrugging his shoulders, palms upturned.

Shirley, husband George in tow, arrived. Rabbit left the group and joined them on the deck at the back of the house.

The police left and the onlookers disappeared. The news spread throughout the village. Robberies were infrequent in Bathsheba and there was a lot of sympathy for the Fielders.

Peter and Monica arrived around 11 o'clock. "I have to tell you that any possible insurance claim might be prejudiced as it appears that the sliding door may have been left unlocked and there was no sign of forced entry," Monica said to Brad and Cindy.

"There are ways to open these types of doors without leaving any evidence," Cindy pointed out. "These doors are not the most secure. In America that would make it a homeowner's liability, especially if there was no kind of bar to inhibit the door from sliding. So I think we might have a good claim."

"We will report it and see what the insurers say," said Monica.

Brad raised the question of whether the rest of the family should abandon the holiday and return home as soon as possible but he was alone in that opinion. And any way Bud and Norma, Cindy's parents, were flying in the next afternoon.

They decided to cancel their luncheon engagement. Instead Cindy and Kathy would stop by for breakfast in Chancery Lane after taking Brad to the airport in the morning.

"Why don't you spend the day with us until you pick up Brad and Norma? You'll be near the airport. Kathy could go windsurfing, it's nearby," said Monica.

They agreed and Peter and Monica said their goodbyes. Brad started packing as soon as they left. He had a very early flight the next morning.

About 5 o'clock that evening Sam Rice came by the house. He only heard of the robbery when he got off the bus and he understood that people were calling his name and the police wanted to question him. "It is a good thing I wasn't even in Bathsheba last night."

Brad was sympathetic. He told Sam that he should be prepared to answer questions about the source of the funds he paid them. Sam didn't stay long.

The next morning they were up early to see Brad off. Cindy drove him to the airport. A bleary eyed Kathy accompanied them. The girls said their goodbyes to Brad and headed to the Devonishes for breakfast. Kathy was excited about the opportunity to windsurf. Cindy decided she would head back to Bathsheba after breakfast. It was Shirley's day off and she wanted to have things ready for her parents' arrival. She would return for Kathy on the way to the airport.

About ten minutes after Cindy returned to Bathsheba, Sam Coochie approached *Casa de Carlos*, a new painting under one arm and a canvas bag over his shoulder. He entered the property from the rear and slid the unlocked sliding door open. Cindy lay curled on the bed, reading a book. Sam entered the room. He held the painting in both hands and said, "This is for you."

Cindy got up off the bed and tossed a brown paper bag to Sam.

"Here, this is for you," she said.

Sam caught the paper bag with one hand. A smile broke out on his face. He rested the painting on the floor, put the paper bag in the canvas bag and rested it next to the painting. He turned, Cindy's arms encircled his neck and she buried her head in his chest. Sam ran his fingers through her curly brown hair. His strong arms easily lifted her plump figure. He slowly spun her around and laid her on the bed.

A Dog's Tale

I heard the sound of the car as it eased its way up the hill. I knew that sound apart from that of any other car, even if it was the same make and model, so I ran to the gate. I was so happy to see him and I knew that he was happy to see me. He opened the gate and I jumped up trying to put my front paws on his shoulders but he put out his hands and caught my paws. I am as tall as he is when I stand on my hind legs. He doesn't like me to dirty his clothes. He is a sharp dresser, an important man, a headmaster of a school, I have heard people say. I heard him say, "One must always look the part, you know." He was wearing a long sleeved shirt with gold cuff links and a tie with matching gold tie-pin. The creases on his trousers looked sharp enough to cut. His brown shoes were so shiny I could see myself in them. I am nearly the same colour as his shoes but with a reddish tint.

He danced with me a little then got back in the car. He drove slowly up the concrete pathway to the carport at the side of the house. I kept pace with the car, jumping at the window. He got out of the car and said," I am going to feed you soon, Ella." That's what they call me, Ella, after a lady he likes to hear sing. He plays her music often and I like to hear her sing too. She makes beautiful sounds, just like us. I mean she just doesn't sing words. She makes wonderful sounds. He calls it scatting. So now when they tell me to stop howling, I tell myself they don't appreciate my sdogging. He climbed the three steps and entered the house through the open door from the carport. I heard him talking to Mavis. She cooks and cleans for my people. He wanted to know what was for dinner and Mavis said, "I cook a lil' beef soup wid dumplins and sweet-potato and ponkin." She meant pumpkin but that is how she talks. Mavis is sweet. She likes me. She feeds me treats during the day. I learned my Bajan dialect from her and my English from Jaycee.

Jaycee brought my food and some water to the carport which Mavis calls, "De garage." He had changed his clothes. He still looked sharp in his khaki shorts and shirt-jac and slippers. I followed him to my eating place at the back of the carport. He said, "Sit." I sat until he poured the water into one bowl and emptied the food into my other bowl. He said, "Eat." I dove into my bowl of rice and bone meal.

As soon as I finished eating, I heard Dot's car and I ran to the gate. Jaycee followed me to the gate and opened it. She drove through and we followed. He held on to my collar, trying to stop me from welcoming her properly. But when she got out of the car, she came over and rubbed her hand over my head and tickled me under my chin. "How is my girl?" she asked. I barked twice and she understood that to mean I am fine.

He calls her Dot and she calls him Jaycee but some people call her, Dorothy and him, John. She is no dot, though. She is taller and bigger than he is and always has her hair swept back into a bun. She is what Mavis calls, "a nice brown-skin lady." They entered the house and I stretched out on the landing just outside. It is one of my favourite spots. My favourite spots are nearest to where ever my family inside the house is, at any time. If they are in the dining room, I stretch out on this landing. If they are in the sitting room, I am on the veranda. It's a big veranda with three Berbice chairs and a big coffee table on either side of the centered double doors. In the morning the veranda is shaded by the big mango tree. When they are in the bed rooms, I am outside the window, either in the shade of the pear tree which some of our friends from overseas call avocado, or at the back of the house lying on the concrete slab that covers the well. From there I can look out over the roof tops below and down to the sea.

"Callie's late again," said Jaycee.

"Oh, I am sure she'll be home soon. I wouldn't worry," replied Dot.

"Uh, oh, here they go again. I think I will go and wait for Callie." I slowly got up and ambled down toward the gate. The dog next door, on the other side of the high fence that separated us from the Bradshaws, called out to me. I answered him but kept going to the gate. He likes me but Jaycee doesn't like to see me talking to him. He calls him that *m-word* all the time. He has a wonderful name, Shaka. But even that is a problem for Jaycee. Everything on the other side of the fence is a problem for Jaycee. Jaycee may have a point about my friend's name, though. I mean, he is not an African dog like me. He is what Jaycee calls a *m-word*. But he is a beautiful dog, brown with white patches and floppy ears and he is big, nearly as big as me. He says nice things to me. He admires the inverse ridge of hair down the centre of my back. I tell him that is because I am a Ndebele lion-dog, a *simba-inja*, as Jaycee likes to tell me. My forebears hunted lions. In this fenced-in garden, I just get to chase the odd rat or mongoose or monkeys when they come to tease me or to eat the mangoes, golden apples, pears or bananas.

I sat by the gate for a good while, looking through the two-inch square galvanized wire at the traffic as it went by. Here she comes, my Callie and she is with Rommel from next door. She is going to be in big trouble. She said good-bye to Rommel outside the gate. She held his hand briefly before he went on his way. She watched him go, a hand on the gate, then she flipped the V-shaped hinged latch on top of the gate, rushed in and grabbed hold of me. I was shaking my tail so hard it shook my whole backside. She fell to her knees, laughing and asked me if I missed her. "Dah is a kreshtun?" as Mavis would say or, "Yuh axsing ef?" I rolled over on my back and I didn't have to tell her to tickle me. I wished she could understand what I wanted to tell her. I walked with her into the carport. She entered the house and I stretched out on the landing which Mavis calls, "de top step."

As soon as she said, "hello mom, hello dad," Jaycee started.

"You are late again, young lady."

"I was in the library and the time went by, I didn't realise."

"You have a cell phone. Why didn't you call?"

"Oh, Dad, I am only an hour late. Why the fuss?"

"An hour and a half, actually. Was that Rommel Bradshaw I saw with you?"

"Rommel waited for me. We came home on the bus together. You should start trusting me, you know."

Dot intervened. "Go and wash your hands sweetheart and come back and have something to eat."

Dot continued as soon as Callie left the room. "Jaycee, you are too hard on that girl. Take care you don't drive her to what you want to drive her away from."

"I only want good things for my child. If she had buckled down and done some work she might have gotten a scholarship, like her brother. And that boy, Rommel, he doesn't seem like a bad boy but he is a Bradshaw, a truck driver's son. She can do better. We have to talk her out of this, this, whatever it is. I thought she liked that Worrell boy who won a scholarship the same year as Jason and is studying medicine. And I don't like the way she has been dressing here of late. She has outgrown those tee-shirts."

They stopped talking as Callie came back into the room and sat at the table. "I want to ask you a question, Calpurnia," Jaycee said, as soon as he raised his head after prayers.

Uh,oh, this is trouble. She doesn't like to be called Calpurnia. I saw Callie look away, out the window toward the sea. But I didn't think she was checking out the view. She gritted her teeth and turned to face her dad.

"Why do you insist on calling me that name? Isn't it bad enough that you saddled me with it so that kids at school can tease me?"

"I am impressed that your fellow students recognise the name Calpurnia. You have a beautiful name."

I've heard this one before. I knew exactly what he was going to say. They named her Juliette Calpurnia Downes. Dot chose Juliette and Jaycee chose Calpurnia. Jaycee insisted she be called Calpurnia but Dot and everyone in the village and at school just called her Callie.

"Your mother and her friends corrupted your name." There, he said it.

I can't listen to this anymore; it is *day-Jah-view*, as Jaycee enjoyed repeating what one of his former students once wrote in class. I slipped away and went in search of my friend next door, the wonderful Shaka. He was waiting for me. As time goes by, I like him more and more. If only that fence wasn't there we could be together. We rubbed noses through the fence. I started whining uncontrollably. I didn't know what was happening to me. I felt the blood rushing through my veins. Then I heard Callie calling me, calling me, "Ella, Ella, where's my doggie?" I turned and loped across the grass in the direction of her voice. She was sitting on the top step of the veranda. She hugged me and said that her dad thought she was still a little girl. Poor girl, I felt sorry for her. She wanted to know where I had been, why didn't I come as soon as she called. I stayed with her a little but I wanted to go back to my friend. She sensed, clever girl, and let me go. I dashed back to the wire and to Shaka.

The next morning is what they call Saturday; I don't understand why a day has to have a name. But then, sometimes people are a complete mystery to me, strange indeed. I was on de top step in the carport. Jaycee and Dot were having breakfast. I had mine already. I always get to eat before them.

"Last night Calpurnia said that Ella is in heat," said Jaycee.

In heat? What is he talking about? What does he mean? Callie never said any such thing to me.

"I don't want her mating with that mongrel next door. I phoned Walter Manning and he said to bring her up to the plantation this morning. He wants to cross her with a Rottweiler. He says that Rottweilers and Rhodesian Ridgebacks make lovely pups."

What is he talking about? I ran around to the other side of the house outside of Callie's bedroom. She was on her cell phone. "We really have to talk. Why don't you come over after my parents leave, they will be gone for about an hour and a half." She kept on talking. I ran back around to the carport. Chairs scraped on the tiled floor in the dining room. They have finished breakfast. I stood at the door and Jaycee came out and said, "We are taking you for a drive this morning, Ella." Now I like to go for a drive. I like to sit in the back seat on my special towel and put my head at the window and feel that breeze and look at the trees and houses and people. But I was worried and anxious. I barked at him, again and again. I wished they could understand me the way I understood them.

I ran to the fence and Shaka came running over. I told him what I thought was happening. He told me we should jump the fence and run away. I am tempted to try but decide "not me and dat." Then Jaycee and Dot came looking for me. I wanted to run away but I told myself that they would never do anything to harm me. I walked with them to the car and we set off. But today I was not enjoying the drive. We drove for a long time and we ended up high in the hills.

Wait, hang on. This place looks familiar and that man coming down the steps with that ugly dog looks familiar. He turned his head. I saw the long blond hair combed over the bald patch, the sun-burnt skin with reddish patches and the long nose, it was Wally. This is where I lived before I went to the Downes' house. Oh, I was happy to see old Wally, but what an ugly dog. We parked under the old evergreen tree and we got out of the car. I ran up to old Wally and sniffed him. He was happy to see me.

"She is a beautiful dog," he said. "She and Duke will make excellent pups."

Duke, who the hell is Duke? Not that ugly thing that's eyeing me up and is sniffing at me? Not in a month of Saturdays. I wanted to go home. Jaycee started to talk to me. "Now, come on, girl." Duke kept coming around the back of me and trying to climb on top of me. But I kept shifting and Jaycee kept trying to hold me. I kept my tail between my legs and Jaycee tried to lift it up. "Now come on, girl," he said.

Eventually, old Wally said, "I think we'd better try this another time. I don't really think she is in heat."

Thank you, Wally, thank you. We got back in the car and Dot was laughing her head off. Jaycee was upset; he didn't think it was funny. "Oh, yeah," said Dot, "you didn't see yourself, a grown man trying to force a seventy pound dog into a sex act." Even I started to laugh.

As we approached our house, suddenly I heard Jaycee let out his breath, "What is he doing coming out of our gate?" The car sped up then braked sharply. Jaycee flung open the door and shouted at Rommel, "I want a word with you." Rommel opened his gate and as he did so, Shaka saw me and ran out of the gate. I made for the open car-door. Jaycee's head swiveled and his body tried to do the same. I heard him yelp, "Oh, my ankle." I saw him fall. Let's run into the woods Shaka told me. Shaka ran across the road into the woods. But Jaycee was on the ground, in pain. I wanted to go with Shaka but I couldn't leave Jaycee.

Callie came out of the house and Dot called out, "Go bring a towel with ice, quick."

Rommel came over and lifted Jaycee to his feet. He put Jaycee's arm around his neck and they did a three-legged walk up to the veranda. I followed them. Rommel settled Jaycee into a Berbice chair, swung the leg extensions outward and lifted the injured leg on to one of them. Jaycee raised the other leg on to the other extension. Callie arrived with towel and ice and applied it to the injured ankle. Rommel turned and walked away.

"Thank you," shouted Jaycee. Rommel just kept on walking. He closed the gate behind him and flipped the V-shaped latch hard. "Come, Shaka," he said. I didn't even know that Shaka was at the gate.

"What was he doing here, with you, alone?" asked Jaycee.

"I invited him over," said Callie. She took her hands off the towel and looked at her father. "I wanted to talk to him, to tell him how I really felt about him. But you know what? He just wants to be my friend. He is not interested in me as a girlfriend. I don't understand."

Jaycee winced but I am not sure if it was the pain in his ankle or if it was the thought of his daughter being rejected by a Bradshaw. Then he started to laugh until Dot gave him one of her stares.

I walked away quietly. They don't even see me go. People are strange, I told myself. I went to the back of the house and sat on the concrete slab over the well and looked out over the roof tops, out to sea.

❧ ❦

The PTA Meeting

Ernestine Chandler paused to watch the group of children having a kick-around on the school playing field, an informal game of football. There was a smile on her narrow face, a smile that lingered perhaps by memories of a youth long gone. She watched the boys and girls, running and laughing and yelling at each other, enjoying themselves as only children can. The group of adults watching seemed to be having almost as much fun, their pleasure vicarious but so obvious.

A girl, she could be no more than ten years old, with corn-rowed hair who seemed to be running all the time, hit a scooped shot which went over the goalie's head and through the bars. There was uproar as the onlookers cheered and shouts of "Goal, goal, goal" erupted around the playing field. The goal scorer cartwheeled with joy and the skill of an acrobat in the making.

Ernestine waved at Julius, the old security guard sitting in the shade on the far side. She turned and hurried away in the direction of her intended destination, the classroom at the far end. She passed the motley set of single-storey buildings constructed of unpainted concrete breeze blocks, those near the roof set on their side to permit constant airflow. Metal piping supported the roof extensions over the outdoor walkways and galvanized sheeting covered the roof.

God, what ugly buildings, was the recurring thought each time Ernestine entered the school environs. Perhaps they were designed by children. Then she caught herself: children would have done a better job.

When she entered the classroom the meeting had just started. There was still room in the front row. She sat centre front and welcomed the light cross breeze that flowed through the open metal louvre windows. At least the architects did get this part right, she thought. She looked around the room and wondered why many of the others avoided the front row.

She did not speak on any of the agenda items. She felt that eyes were on her and from time to time she turned her head. And yes, there was always someone looking at her.

"Wait, Miss Chandler like she ain't saying nothing today. What happen?" The loud whisper reached Ernestine's ears.

The meeting neared its end. "That completes our agenda," said the chairperson, Mrs. Boyce, matter-of-factly.   "Is there any other business?" Mrs. Boyce was a formidable-looking woman, seemingly always confident and in control. Her plump figure belied an energy level not associated with someone her size. She paused after the question and peered over half glasses, perched on her wide, fleshy nose, at the members of the St. Agnes Primary School PTA. She spoke from a head table, flanked by the headmistress, treasurer, secretary and Reverend Farley, vicar of the nearby St. Agnes Church. Assembled before her was a small group of parents and teachers, more or less the same group who always attended PTA meetings, unless there was some particular problem to be discussed.

Ernestine raised her hand.

"Yes, Mrs. Chandler."

Ernestine stood. The eyes in the room turned in her direction. Some eyes rolled or looked to the ceiling. Sarcasm laden smiles spread across some faces. They knew her as someone who always had a complaint. Often it was her health, in spite of her spritely appearance, or just life in general. If you said to Ernestine, "It is a lovely day," you risked starting a conversation on all the things that could possibly go wrong as the day progressed.

Each of her six children had attended St. Agnes Primary and her youngest was still there. At times she could be a real bother to the administration but her support of their activities was exemplary. She was a keen volunteer for fairs, sports days and any other school event.

"Madame Chairwoman, let me get straight to the point. I understand that the Barbados *Mirror* is in the school library every day for our children to read. Am I correct, Madame Chairwoman?" She spoke in a high-pitched voice and the veins stood out on her long neck.

Mrs. Boyce lowered her grey-streaked head to peer over her half glasses and with a nod to the headmistress deflected the question toward her for a response.

"You are correct, Mrs. Chandler" said Ms. Cadogan, a broad-shouldered, athletic-looking woman. Many a student, past and present, on the receiving end of corporal punishment from her, could testify to her strength. "We wish that our children should have the opportunity to keep abreast of current affairs and they have shown an interest in discovering what is going on in the country and the wider world. The news items make interesting points for discussion."

Around the room heads were nodding in agreement but Ernestine Chandler's was not one of them. She looked at the nodding heads and the look of determination on her face hardened. She reached into her old canvas bag and pulled out a wad of newspaper clippings.

She selected one of the clippings and held it up. She handed it to the man on her right. "Look at this and pass it around. This is the kind of things our children will see when they look in the Mirror." The clipping showed a photo from the stage of a Crop Over calypso tent. A woman with a rather large backside and a broad grin was bent over with a man behind her in a dance which could be considered a simulated sexual act. "You want to hear a joke?" Mrs. Chandler said. "Children are not allowed in these calypso tents, but we can put this newspaper in our schools for the children to see some woman pooching back on a man."

She selected another clipping, this one of a flimsily-costumed female Kadooment reveller on the ground, face down and a costumed man on top of her, faces on the surrounding crowd beaming. "Look at this, look at this!" She passed this one to her left. "Pass it on, pass it on. *Please.* I want everybody to see these." She pulled more newspaper clippings from her bag. One headline boldly declared, "Woman cuts off man's penis."

One of the parents, a man with a full neatly trimmed beard, whispered to the lady next to him, "That is old news. What she keep that newspaper so long for?" He steupsed and turned toward the head table. Ernestine turned in his direction but addressed the room.

"I only get the papers on a Sunday and I have to cut these out before my little children get a chance to look at them. I ain't got as much education as some of the people in this room but I got good old common sense. Look at this now." She started to toss more clippings around calling out the headlines as she distributed them. "Is this what we want to expose our children to? I want this newspaper removed from the school library."

The photo of the couple at the calypso tent reached the whisperer who Ernestine had overheard earlier. He exclaimed, "Wait, that is Cammie granddaughter. The apple don't fall far from the tree for true, eh heh."

"Yes, she is somebody's daughter, Mr. Bourne, somebody's daughter, and these newspapers can't find anything better to print," said Ernestine, throwing a hand in the air.

"Mrs. Chandler has a point," announced Reverend Farley from the head table.

"Oh, Lordie, if the reverend start we going be here till the frogs start whistling," said the whisperer, looking straight ahead and speaking out of the side of his mouth.

"Just a moment, Reverend," the headmistress interrupted, cutting him off before he could get into stride. "The children will get exposed to all of these things anyway. It is certainly better that they read about them than experience them. And it is better that they find out about them in school, where they can ask questions and have these things properly explained by teachers."

Some of the nodders nodded but not as many as before. People were talking from the floor and the head table at the same time. Mrs. Boyce did not call them to order immediately. She tried to listen to all the comments. Reverend Farley raised his voice in earnest reply.

"From the time of Adam and Eve, parents have been complaining about their children. But parents don't seem to accept any responsibility for the behaviour of the very offspring that they brought into this world. The loudest complaints come from the present generation of parents. The children this, the children that. But what about the parents?" He pounded on the head table and scanned the room as if he was asking everyone there for a response. There was silence.

"You have made an interesting point, Reverend, parental responsibility is of utmost importance," said Mrs. Boyce.

The parents started to talk among themselves.

"Order, order, please."

The whisperer stood up to speak. The novelty of this act brought silence to the room. He looked down at his shoes then up to the head table, cleared his throat loudly and spoke quietly. "I agree with Mistress Chandler. We don't want our children reading this kind of thing." He sat as soon as the words were out of his mouth.

"You really think that you can shield children from information in this day and age, this age of 24-hour TV and the Internet?" said Ms. Cadogan. "Don't you know they call this the Information Age? You should see some of the text messages these children send to each other. You didn't see some of them dancing at the last school fair? They are not as innocent as you think."

Ernestine Chandler jumped to her feet. "They are innocent. Innocent until adults corrupt them. My daughter did not learn to dance like that in my house." She looked around the room and saw raised eyebrows, smirks, smiles and nodding heads.

"Please permit me to come in here," said Reverend Farley, standing up as he spoke. "This is not about the Internet and what children can see there. It is about what they can see in their school. It is also about how our newspapers ought to be serving our public...."

"Thank you, Reverend. Ladies and gentlemen, we have started a very interesting discussion and it is a pity that there are so few parents here this evening," said Mrs. Boyce, turning away from a discussion with Mrs. Cadogan. "We think that this should be put to the vote at a specially convened meeting of a larger group of parents, at a date to be announced subsequently."

Reverend Farley sat. He turned toward Ms. Boyce, wagged a finger and said, "I will talk to you after the meeting."

Ernestine raised her hand. "I just want to say one more thing, Mrs. Boyce, when you look in the Mirror..." She stopped, everyone's attention drawn to yelling from the playing field.

The door to the room flew open. One of the boys from the playing field and the girl with the corn-rowed hair rushed into the room.

"They fighting out there, Mrs. Cadogan," one yelled.

"Mark father beating Shanieka mother," shouted the other.

Reverend Farley jumped to his feet. Mrs. Cadogan moved swiftly toward the door, Mrs. Chandler right behind her. Chairs and tables toppled in the rush to follow them. Mrs. Boyce picked up her mobile phone and rapidly pressed numbers. "Police? Hello ... ."

On the playing field, Julius, the guard, lay stretched out on the grass, a woman bent over him, fanning his face slowly with a folded newspaper. "I alright," he said.

Mark's father and Shanieka's mother had been separated but they continued to shout at each other.

"Your child kick mine."

"It wasn't for purpose, you idiot. You shunna gone and hit my child. You is a big able man."

The adults all talking at once, encircled the combatants. Ernestine Chandler turned to Mrs. Boyce, just as she joined the rest of the group.

"And they blame the children," she said.

Iron Man Jones

Geraldine Straughan, editor of the *Daily Standard* newspaper, sat back in her leather chair, fingers clasped over her stomach. She peered over her glasses and with raised eyebrows asked her question.

"Sheri, you want to go all that way to interview someone we interviewed a week ago?" It was only a twenty-minute trip by car but any distance approaching a half hour's drive in Barbados was considered long.

"We didn't really interview him," Sheri replied. "There were more photographs than article. We need a different approach to these stories. Centenarians are repositories of vast amounts of information, not just of family history, how many children and grandchildren they produced. This will be the interview that we should have done. Just think of the history that this man has lived through. Our readers would definitely be interested in the stories that Iron Man Jones can tell."

Iron Man Jones had achieved some notoriety as a crime fighter and an amateur boxer in his youth. Eventually he disappeared into quiet retirement. It was the publicity surrounding the Governor-General's visit on his hundredth birthday that brought him to the attention of Sheri Gooding and the public again. Such visits were the most frequently performed task by the Governor-General in a country with the second highest number of centenarians per capita in the world. At the *Standard* they were usually covered by junior reporters.

Mrs. Straughan still wavered. She recalled arguments with the police commissioner after two particular stories Sheri had written.

"The police are still upset with us over your story on favourite weapons of gang members."

"That's because government officials kept denying there were any gangs in Barbados. Instead of being upset, the police should have focussed on the clues in the photos, the hands, the rings, the jewellery, the clothing. I was doing them a favour."

"And that was after your lifestyle feature on big dogs and their owners. You had us all fooled especially with all the detail on the breeds of the dogs. First we had our competition calling to say we had copied their idea by featuring dogs and their owners. But then the commissioner of police called to complain that the three men you described as businessmen and photographed with the dogs, were all suspected drug dealers."

"The story was about the dogs. But you know what is interesting; none of these drug lords had ever been arrested. And this newspaper, to its shame, did not report the commissioner's comments."

"His comments were off the record, Sheri, you know that. And now you want to interview this legend of the police force."

Sheri bit her lower lip. Iron Man Jones would have retired before this commissioner entered the Police Training School. "I can't imagine why the commissioner would have an issue with this story," she said.

"Sheri, there is something you must understand. The celebration of one hundred years on this earth always has to be a good-news story. My concern is not so much the reaction of the police as the reaction of the public. Centenarians are adored here. I have to tell you, this newspaper will not involve itself in any attempt to disturb the peace that this very old man deserves."

"Ah, but what if that peace is not deserved?" Sheri immediately regretted the question. She raised her hand and quickly continued, "M'am, let me do the interview. After you have heard the recording, let us have this conversation again."

As she left Bridgetown and the suburbs behind, Sheri began to enjoy the drive into the countryside. The canes were in bloom and she watched seas of cane arrows waving in the air, pushed then released over and over again by brisk breezes. Her thoughts alternated between appreciation of the scenery and her impending encounter with Iron Man Jones. She wondered how he would respond to her. Had he now lost some of his legendary iron will? Should she change her style of questioning to one that was less direct and confrontational?

As she crested Horse Hill, the hills and valleys of the East Coast unfolded ahead and the wild waters of the Atlantic came into view. Sheri smiled. She had not been to Bathsheba often. As a child her grandmother had always warned her about the dangerous ocean currents there.

When she reached the outskirts of Bathsheba she recognized her destination, a pink bungalow on the left of a steep hill. It typified the architecture of the Barbadian wall-house: a single-storey, gabled-roof, stone structure with a quarter of the front serving as a gallery.

In the gallery sat an old man. As Sheri exited her Suzuki, he rose from his chair and stood his full six-foot, two inches, a stern expression on his face. He moved with surprising ease for someone his age. A cream shirt-jac hung loosely on his lean frame. What remained of his hair was grey and cut very short. Behind turtleshell-rimmed glasses, piercing eyes followed Sheri as she made her way up the four steps and entered the gallery. She was dressed in a navy blue skirt suit, her salon locks tied neatly behind her neck. She carried her few extra pounds well. A gap-toothed smile broke from her round face as she shifted her bag to her left hand and extended her right hand.

"I am Sheri Gooding. You must be Iron Man Jones. Thanks for agreeing to meet with me."

"You too young to know me by that name. Nowadays, everybody just call me Jones or Jonesie," the tall man replied in a deep voice, glowering as he firmly but gently shook her hand. His speech was slow but his voice was strong, so strong that Sheri wondered if he was a bit deaf.

Jones eyed Sheri. "Your paper interviewed me already. Why you want to interview me again?"

Sheri put on her best smile and said, "Well, Mr. Jones, the *Standard*'s previous interview focused more on the celebration of your hundredth birthday and the Governor-General's visit. From what I have heard there is a lot more to be written about your extraordinary life. After all, you were no ordinary policeman; you were a famous crime fighter and a boxer besides being a family man."

There was a flicker of a smile on Jones' face. "Ah, you heard about my days in the ring. If I'd been born in America, I would have been the heavyweight champion of the world. I was a great counter-puncher. That's when I was most dangerous." He raised his arms, adopted a boxing stance and threw a few feeble, playful punches. He tossed back his head and laughed then pointed to a chair on the opposite side of a low, glass-topped, wrought-iron table. "Have a seat, young lady."

"Thank you," Sheri said as she settled in the chair. She placed her bag on the table and proceeded to take out her digital recorder, writing pad and pencil. Agitated barking erupted from the other side of the road. Sheri turned around to see what was happening. "It's those monkeys again," Jones said. "They won't keep out of Albertine mango tree. They drive the dogs crazy."

"Look, a monkey just threw a mango at one of the dogs," said Sheri, getting up out of her chair. "Oh, that's not fair; monkeys have such an advantage over dogs."

"Girl, you watching a battle between two of the smartest creatures on God's earth. The monkeys may have an advantage, it's true, but they don't always win, you know," said Jones, smiling with a glint in his eyes. "They come right into this gallery sometimes." He looked around then added, "My daughter likes monkeys. She feeds them, leaves bananas on this table for them."

"And do you like monkeys, too, Mr. Jones?"

"They are a pest. I used to shoot them for a friend who was a farmer and could not keep them off his land."

"Really."

The plump, smiling figure of Jones' youngest daughter, Erma, entered the gallery carrying a tray with refreshments. Erma and her husband moved in with her father fourteen years ago, after the passing of his beloved Babsie. On the tray were two glasses of freshly made lemonade and four slices of coconut bread. She introduced herself and said with a giggle, "I take care of him, now. All this talk will make you thirsty."

She left the tray on the low table and disappeared back inside the house.

"Before we start," said Sheri, "I must tell you I enjoyed what little we printed about your life. I was fascinated when you said that as a child you were licks-proof."

They both laughed. Sheri turned on her recorder.

"Mr. Jones, did that early severe childhood discipline influence your decision to become a policeman?"

Jones smiled. He straightened his shoulders, inhaled deeply, exhaled through flared nostrils and said, "You could say that was part of the reason. But you know what was more important? It was steady employment. If I was a carpenter or mason, when I finish one job, I would be out of work until I find a next one. And work could be hard to come by in those days. Things were hard, hard then. You understand?"

He spoke in slow, clear, deliberate sentences and moved both hands in some kind of disorganized sign language.

"How did you earn your reputation as a tough policeman?"

Jones laughed. "Simple, I enforced the law. And anyway, in those days, policemen were big, strapping men. People respected policemen."

"You say respected, but I understand that people were afraid of you. Was that so?"

Jones scowled a little. It seemed like an act to Sheri. "No, no, no, miss, people wasn't afraid of me. Only criminals was afraid of me." He wagged a finger, leaned forward a little and continued in a raised voice: "You see, I never used to give up when I was hunting down a criminal…."

"Surely you mean a suspect," interrupted Sheri.

The scowl intensified on Jonesie's face. He lowered his gaze and looked askance at Sheri without speaking. Then that flicker of a smile returned to his face and he said loudly, wagging his finger again in Sheri's direction, "You know what is wrong with people like you? You never been a victim of a crime. Nobody never grabble you and drag you in the bush and violate you and leave you there like a piece o' nutten."

Erma's face appeared at the little side window, the one to the right of the door. Sheri looked at her and smiled a strained smile. Erma smiled back, sighed and retreated.

"Mr. Jones, I was just making the point that in our system of justice a person is innocent until proven guilty."

Jones caressed his chin between thumb and forefinger, chuckled and performed a little upward nod of his head. "That is before the courts, young lady. That is our court system. The courts don't recognize guilt until it is proven to the satisfaction of a judge and jury, and that is the way it should be. I don't have a problem with that, but you have to separate judicial guilt from real guilt." He kept waving that finger. His slowness of speech was the only real indicator of his age.

"But for me, a person is guilty the moment they commit a crime. They are guilty in the eyes of the victim, they are guilty in their own conscience," he said, thrusting a forefinger at his temple, "and your conscience is the voice of God. That is why, when I know a man commit a crime, I went after him with everything I got."

"What do you mean with everything?" Sheri sat back in her chair without taking her eyes off Jones. "Might that include beating a suspect?"

His eyes narrowed and he stared unblinking at Sheri. His pursed lips twitched a little, but he said nothing. Sheri would have liked to take a picture of him at that moment. A large vein stood out on his round forehead. His pouted mouth was set. His face registered his emotions like a seismograph. She resisted reaching into her bag for the camera fearing it might have ended the interview. She picked up her pencil and scribbled in her pad instead.

"Young lady, I don't know what you hear, but let me tell you something. I, Carlisle Athelston Jones," he said thumping his chest twice with his right fist, "never…never raise a hand against nobody… that wasn't threatening me. But if you attack me, you better know which God you serving." He leaned forward and spoke slowly and clearly. "Because you will want to talk to Him."

He straightened up and gave Sheri that stare again. "I had a different way of dealing with criminals. When a fellow didn't want to talk, I used to put him in a holding cell at the station and he would not eat nor drink till he ready to talk to me. After a few hours, I would draw up a chair in front the cell door and sit down with a glass of mauby and a cheese cutter. I would start to eat slow, slow, asking a quiet question in between each bite. No lot of fuss, no threats, no beating, but he would start talking."

There was a moment of silence in the gallery. Sheri scribbled in her notepad and looked up to see Jones' eyes focused on her.

"Mr. Jones, I would like to ask you about your role in the riots of 1937."

Sheri waited and watched. Jones' face told her that memories were racing through his head. Memories of her research into the riots flashed through her mind.

In July 1937 there was an uprising in Barbados. Citizens mired in abject poverty rioted over a four-day period. The spark that ignited the riots was the deportation of Clement Payne. Payne was a Marxist political activist who had been sent by his party in Trinidad to spread the word in his parents' native Barbados. The oppressive living conditions of working-class Barbadians were perfect for Payne's task and he was perfect for the job. He was handsome, charismatic and a brilliant orator. He held a series of meetings which attracted large crowds. He also attracted the attention of the authorities.

The authorities arrested Payne. They charged him with falsifying his entry papers into Barbados. He was convicted. But on appeal, represented by a promising young lawyer named Grantley Adams, he was acquitted. The authorities responded by surreptitiously shipping Payne back to Trinidad. The people responded by rioting.

The riots were swiftly put down. There were street battles between armed policemen and rioters. Crowds attacked stores and other business places but much of their anger was vented at the black police force who were under the direction of white officers and charged with protecting white-owned property. The police won those battles and a reputation for cruelty which would linger for years.

Jones picked up a piece of coconut bread and took a bite then took a sip of lemonade. He looked at the dogs and monkeys on the other side of the road, and in a quiet voice, accompanied by a wave of his hand, said, "I don't wish to talk about any riots. You can read the Moyne Commission report if you want information about the riots."

"I have read The West Indies Royal Commission Report," said Sheri, using the report's rarely used formal name, "but the thoughts and recollections of a living witness, even though it is seventy years after the event, would be of great interest to our readers."

"I don't want to talk about no riots. You understand?"

Sheri looked down at the table then looked up again and asked, "Did you read the Moyne report, Mr. Jones?"

Jones raised his voice. "No."

"Why not, may I ask?"

"Because I lived it. You think the Moyne report could tell me anything that I did not already know? I lived through those times. All my family was as poor as the people pelting rocks." He spoke loudly.

Sheri persisted. "So you understood the reasons your fellow citizens rioted. You understood the hopelessness of those people?"

The centenarian stared at Sheri, piercing eyes searching her face.

"Young lady, I keep telling you I don't want to talk about no riots." He spoke calmly again but there was anger in his eyes.

Sheri took a sip of lemonade, put down her glass. "Wouldn't you like the chance to defend yourself about some of the things that people have said about you, and how you conducted yourself then?"

Jones stared at Sheri through squinted eyes.

"I know what people say 'bout me and...and about other policemen, too. But we had a job to do, and that was to restore law and order. We din want to kill nobody." He was speaking faster now. "Look, we shoot off hundreds of rounds and only fourteen people get kill. Why you think that is? And I goin' tell you something now that nobody never write 'bout: the police was not the only people shooting! We wasn't the only people with guns. That is all I have to say, that is all I have to say."

"Who else did the shooting, Mr. Jones?" asked Sheri swiftly.

Jones' face contorted into a look of incredulity. "You don't know about the men on top the stores in Broad Street, behind the parapets shooting down at the people?"

Sheri's back straightened. She raised her voice. "No. Who were these men?"

Jones steupsed, looked away and then back again.. "I don't know. I wasn't there. I will leave that up to you to find out. You are a reporter. I tell you I have nothing more to say. Don't ask me no more questions about the damn riots."

Sheri scribbled rapidly on the pad in front of her. She got up from her chair. She walked around in a circle. She sensed fear, the fear of a man whose early life was spent in a time of fear.

"You know who they were, don't you?" she asked quietly.

Jones remained silent. He turned his head to the left and looked toward the sea, as determined a profile as Sheri ever saw. This avenue of questioning was closed.

Sheri returned to her seat. She inhaled deeply, then slowly exhaled. "Do you remember a man called Billy Bascombe?" she asked.

Jones head straightened. He recoiled as if he had been thumped in the chest. He looked toward the dogs and monkeys. The dogs were leaping and yapping while the monkeys skipped through the branches of the mango tree, just out of reach.

Iron Man Jones turned to face Sheri. His eyes closed to a squint, nostrils flared, jaw muscles tightened. "What you want to know 'bout Billy Bascombe? That he was a rogue and a vagavun?"

Sheri bent a little closer and looked directly into Jones' eyes. "Was it you who shot him, Mr. Jones?" Sheri could hear his breathing.

His eyes searched her face then he looked away and back again.

"I ain't afraid to admit that I shoot Billy Bascombe. But let me tell you something, I was a marksman; I could hit a sixpence at a hundred yards. If I wanted Billy Bascombe dead, he would be dead the minute he aim the first rock-stone at me."

Iron Man Jones Jones jabbed his finger in Sheri's direction.

"I shoot him in his arm because I didn't want to kill him. He was going to hit me with a rock. He had two rocks in his hands and was cursing me and the police. He called us the king watch-dogs and a bunch of marching monkeys."

42

"You shot him because he called you names?" Sheri demanded.

"Oh, no, I was used to being called names. You know, sometimes a policeman had to be as aggressive as those dogs." He waved his hand in the direction of Albertine's property on the other side of the road. "And other times he had to be as cunning as the monkeys. The names didn't bother me. The rock-stones was my problem. I shoot him in his right arm and he still tried to pelt the rock in his left hand, so I shoot him in his leg and he fall down in the road. I understand that he only end up in a wheelchair because he couldn't get to the hospital right away."

"You mean you shot Billy Bascombe and left him to bleed to death. It was only the bravery of neighbours who pushed him in a box-cart all the way to the hospital that helped him to survive."

She bit her lips to stop them from quivering and rubbed her eyes. She looked away from Iron Man. She thought of the man in the wheelchair and she thought of her editor listening to the tape of this interview. This would surely change her mind about that "age is honour" crap. She turned back to Iron Man, looked directly into his eyes and spoke very slowly.

"Mr. Jones, there is something I want to tell you." She paused and looked at his scarred face, the long healed wounds of fights won and lost, the fiery eyes. "Billy Bascombe was my grandfather."

Iron Man gripped the arms on his chair and started to rise on legs which now seemed rusty. Halfway up, his arms melted and he fell back into his seat. His breathing grew louder and laboured. He called out, "Erma, Erma," but his voice had lost its metal.

Sheri rushed to the door to the living room and shouted for Erma.

"Your father is calling you."

"What is the matter, Daddy?"

Iron Man pointed a shaky finger in Sheri's direction and, trembling, said, "She, she say she is Billy Bascombe granddaughter."

Erma turned to Sheri. A vein stood out on her forehead, from the centre of her hairline to the space above her nose.

"You come here to ambush my father just like Billy Bascombe"

"He crippled my grandfather."

"I live wid them taunts from the time I was a little girl." Erma turned her back to Sheri. "How you feeling, Dad? I think you should come to bed."

"I alright, child, bring me a cup o' sweetment tea."

Erma turned and left the gallery.

Iron Man's breathing had relaxed, but his face appeared drained of blood.

"Your grandmother was Ercil Grant?" he whispered.

"Yes. How do you know?"

Iron Man took off his glasses and ran his right hand over his head, forehead to nape. He inhaled and exhaled loudly, put back on his glasses.

"Billy Bascombe was a good-looking, no-good, thiefing reprobate. Your grandmother was going to get rid of him," he said in a soft voice. "He attacked me because she was going to leave him for me. But after she heard that I shoot him she wouldn't have anything to do with me."

"You knew my grandmother?"

"Yes, I knew Ercil." The piercing eyes looked deep into her skull. "I knew Ercil and I have something to tell you… Billy Bascombe is not your grandfather."

His words reverberated in Sheri's head. She picked up her recorder and turned it off. She rose from the chair, turned and walked to the edge of the gallery and looked across at Albertine's property. The monkeys had gone and the dogs were resting among scattered leaves and half-eaten mangoes, strewn on the ground.

Sheri's head was on fire. Through watery eyes she could see the old man in the wheelchair. He who doted on her for the first ten years of her life, whose face would transform from sad to happy whenever he caught sight of her. She saw her grandmother's face, always serious and sad. Then Sheri thought of her mother, who seemed incapable of keeping secrets from her. No, this could not be true. "This old bastard behind me could not be telling the truth." …But what if he was telling the truth?

She turned swiftly and spat out her words. "You are a blasted liar, Iron Man Jones." She hurled the recorder. Iron Man bobbed but the recorder had already whistled past his left ear. It hit the wall behind him, bounced to the floor and shattered into small pieces on the gallery.

Sheri froze, the back of one hand cupped in the palm of the other and both covering her open mouth. Her scream turned into a wheeze. She stared at Iron Man's face. It was blank, the seismograph turned off. He sat, still as a statue, his eyes fixed on Sheri. Sheri's eyes were blazing and a long, small vein stood out on her forehead.

৵৵

The Train Hopper

Dedicated to the memory of "The Mighty Phoenix"

My littlest great-grands like me to tell them stories about days gone by in Barbados. When they are with me or when I go up to Rowan's in St. George to my granddaughter, these children don't want no bedtime story from a book. They want to hear something from my boy days. Sometimes they don't believe me when I tell them certain things, cause this is a different world altogether from when I was a boy. They laugh when I tell them about people walking from Bathsheba to Bridgetown and back; about bringing a bucket of water on your head; cooking in the backyard in a pot over three rock-stones with a wood fire and all of them kind of things. But today they bringing two friends and they want me tell them about the first time I went hopping the train.

I sit down on the veranda waiting for them and taking the breeze. When that car drive up, they jump out and run up to me and hug me up; make a old man so happy.

Their mother, Grace, tell them, "Don't hug Grandad so tight, you might hurt him."

I lean over and whisper to them, "Don't mind your mother. I like hugs," and Grace give me a big hug, too.

The girl, Shoshanna, she younger than she brother, Thomas, but she bold-faced, introduce me to their two friends. "Grandad, this is Rashida and this is Addissa. They go to school with us and they want to hear about the day you hopped the train from Bathsheba all the way to Bridgetown."

She turn and whisper to her two friends. "You mustn't interrupt grand-dad because you will make him forget." But I hear every word. My ears still good, you know.

Grace gone in the house to look for her aunt. I hear the fridge door open and then the TV turn on. The children sit down at my feet, in a semi-circle on the floor of the verandah, and I start my story.

They laugh out when I tell them that I was a very mischievous child and used to get nuff licks. They only laughing because they don't get none. I tell them that those were hard times and parents didn't used to make no sport with children.

My father hardly ever beat me. He was a mason and when he work far from home, he used to sleep out weeknights and come home weekends. My mother would beat me with anything she could put her hands on at the time. If she was hanging out clothes, she would sting me with a wet shirt; if she was in the little piece of ground behind the house, she would break a switch off a pea tree or some bush and fling it in me. They laugh again. "You only laughing because you don't get no licks. My mother couldn't read nor write; when I was a boy, this was common. Things in Barbados was not like them is now, you understand?" The children look a little sad when I tell them so and their eyes look as if they trying to see into the past.

One of the worst beatings I get, though, was a day I didn't go to school; I spent the day playing cricket and then cray-fishing with some bigger boys in Joe's River. When I get home Ma pick up the coucou stick and lick the pan with the crayfish flying out of my hand. She put a beating pun me that I never forget until the day I went hopping the train.

Some boys in Bathsheba used to hop on the train and ride to Belleplaine or Bath and walk back, but there was a fellow name Thelbert who everybody used to call Baldwin. He used to hop a morning train all the way to Bridgetown and hop an evening one back to Bathsheba. And he would tell us all the stories about the places and things he see. I first see Bridgetown through the eyes of Baldwin. Baldwin was a legend in Bathsheba.

One day during the school vacation, I ain't had nothing to do. I done tie out the two goats, done bring water from the stand-pipe and done clean out the pig pen.

Why you all giggling and looking at one another so?

As I was telling you, I ain't had nothing to do, so I left home to go down to the sea to see if any of my friends was down there. When I reach by the train station there was people waiting for the train, not just passengers. There was always people waiting for the train, old people, young people, people waiting for people, people waiting for things off the train, people just waiting to see people and people waiting to see the train. There was ladies in their long skirts right down to their ankles, all the men was wearing hats and most people was barefoot. I telling you these things because you young people don't know bout life back eighty, ninety years ago.

I stand up near to some men by the train track. Some other men was sitting on the rails. Then I see Baldwin walk up and I know the train coming soon because Baldwin like he could feel the train coming.

"You going town today, Baldwin?" a old man ask.

"That is a question, man?" replied Baldwin, and he turn to me and say, "Why you don't come with me today, young fellow?"

Now I didn't expect Baldwin to ask me so, so I was surprised and excited at the same time. But my mother and a tamarind rod appear in front of my face as if they was real. So I know I couldn't go to town.

You laugh. I was so excited, I just blurt out, "I will go as far as Bath and walk back, Baldwin." And as soon as I say so, I hear the train whistle. Toot-toot. Toot-toot.

It come round the corner, smoke flying from the funnel of the big Baldwin engine. You see, that is how Thelbert got the nickname Baldwin. People got off and away from the tracks. When Baldwin see the train he start to skip around and shout out, "Yes, yes, yes," lashing his fingers together over and over again, like an excited child.

Baldwin tell me, "Now listen to me, young boy. Watch me and do what I do. First thing, check out what in the freight car. If they got barrels of molasses, we ain't going in there because you could get squeeze if they start moving bout. If we got to hang on outside and the train stop going up the hill in St. John, get off to the side. We going help them push it. If the train start to roll back, get out the way fast. Remember the two boys that get kill up there when the train roll back pun them? That would never happen to me. I like to play it safe. And if that foolish idiot, Banfield, working on this train today, you can't come with me because I got to go on top." I remind Baldwin that I only going as far as Bath.

Baldwin went and talk to the guard and I see he pointing at me. I don't know what he tell the conductor but he come and tell me, "We going town today, young boy." Well, we hop on pun this train, and when I reach Bath I was having so much fun that I decide to go all the way to town. At every station, Baldwin helping passengers take off and put on luggage and he tell me to help, too. We pass plantation after plantation and sugar factories. I was surprised at how flat the rest of Barbados was. It ain't like Bathsheba at all.

When we get to Bridgetown, we left the train station and cross the bridge. Baldwin show me Lord Nelson statue. I never see a statue before. But I remember my mother telling me that there was only one Lord and he was invisible. Then we went down the wharf, see men in boats pulling oars and some tall ships in the Careenage. We went all through town; I never see so much people before. There was people everywhere. And I didn't know we had so much white people in Barbados, they all working in town, in banks and stores. I see so many donkey carts and horses with carriages and trams and some motor cars. Everything was for sale, in shops and by hawkers by the side of the road. If you had money, you could buy anything. Town was like another country.

Some people did dress up real purty. Baldwin did know some of the hawkers. A St. Lucian lady give us two mangoes and that is all we eat the whole day. We went back to the station in time for the last train back to Bathsheba.

All my fun was one way that day because on the way back, I just thinking about my mother. I know what in store for me when I get home. When we get back to Bathsheba and I hop off the train I see my friend Bucky Best and he say, "Boy, you going get your tail cut tonight. You mother did looking for you all over Bathsheba, but we ain't tell she nothing."

When I get home I peep through the flaps in the front door and I see a bowl on the table with food in it and a spoon and a tamarind rod next to it. When I see that tamarind rod, I flinch like I taking a lash already. My mother was sitting in a chair next to the partition, fast asleep. I tell myself, "Think, Beresford, think." I thought about running away or climbing through the bedroom window and sneaking into my bed, but I was hungry and the food was in front of me. I was thinking food or licks, food for licks, food and licks; then a idea hit me. We had a lot of rain that year and a lot of people came down with fever from mosquito bites.

I pull open the door and shout out, "Ma, Ma, you hear what happen?"

Ma head jerk off she chest and she shout out, "What happen, boy, wha' happen?"

"You ain't hear that they kill the mosquito that giving all the people fever? The manager at Joe's River Plantation shoot it. It weigh thirty pounds."

The boldfaced little one shout out, "But Grandad, when you told us this story before, the mosquito only weighed twenty pounds."

And her mother shout out from in the house, "And when he first told me that story the mosquito weighed ten pounds."

I ain't pay them no mind. I continue with my story.

Ma look up at the roof, put her hands over her head and she say, "Thank you, Lord, thank you, Jesus." I used to think that the Lord lived on top of our house in those days. "Come and eat your food, boy. Oh, Lord, give me grace." By the way, that is how your mother get her name. My mother was always begging the Lord for grace and your grandmother make her very happy when she name your mother Grace.

Ma went into the bedroom and I sit down and start to eat. I take a pause from eating and pick up that tamarind rod; I break it in two and then break them in two and pelt the pieces out the window.

Ma came out the bedroom and say, "I going down by my sister and come back."

Now, when she say "my sister" and not "your aunt," that shoulda tell me something, because she normally used to say "your aunt" when she talking bout her sister. But I was too hungry to think.

When I finish eating, I was tired so I went and pour some water in a wash pan and went in the yard and wash up. Then I went and curl up in my bed. I fall asleep as soon as my body hit the khus khus and I start to dream. I dream I see a red-hair, freckly face man with a shotgun in his hand and he was outside our house, then this big able mosquito fly in the place. The shotgun follow the mosquito and the mosquito land right on my backside. Before I could move my hand to knock it off, the shotgun went off BRAX and I feel something tear into my backside. I holler out, "Ai, ai, ai, oh Lord, oh Lord." The pain straighten me up, and before I could turn, the window stick tear into my backside again… and again.

My great-grands two little friends' mouths and eyes open wide, wide. My great- grands cackle out but their friends didn't sure if to laugh or not.

The children were quiet for a moment then Shoshanna say, "Tell us another one about the good old days, Grandad."

And I reply, "Next time, dear, next time. You know you only get one story at a time. You must come soon again."

And then the questions start.

෧෧

Breadfruit Brouhaha

The ball bearing wheels droned as Oscar Greaves rolled his box-cart along the Bathsheba coast road. He had made the vehicle himself, out of a wooden box, bits of wood and a pair of used ball bearings. He had pushed the ball bearings on to the ends of a wooden axle nailed to the underside of the box. Next he nailed two strips of wood on opposite sides of the box, diagonally and parallel. He connected them with a cross piece at the top ends to complete the handle of the cart. His finishing touch was two coats of red paint on the outside with four-inch wide green stripes on each side. The box-cart was intended for his work but he took it to the shop for groceries; he did errands for his neighbours and even gave rides to little children.

Box-carts were once common in Barbados, many years ago, but became virtual museum pieces since supermarket trolleys could be acquired. Oscar's box-cart was a crude bit of construction but it did the job of transporting his breadfruits. It replaced the wicker basket he used to carry on his head and earned him a new sobriquet, courtesy of one of the men in Pops', the first time he wheeled the box-cart past the rum-shop. Oscar was no longer Crow or Scarecrow; he was now called Oxcart.

Oscar was twelve years old when his mother told him, "You big enough to help me with these breadfruits now." She packed a basket of breadfruits for him and put it on his head. She first put a pad, made of a piece of crocus bag twisted into a circle, on his head to absorb some of the pressure, but his head shook unsteadily with the weight and his neck hurt. He protested but his mother, taking his complaints as unwillingness, shut him up. "You is a big boy now."

On the way to Cattlewash, a nearby upscale area of beach houses for Bridgetown businessman and old plantocrats, Oscar lagged behind his fast-walking mother, who would occasionally turn and shout, "Come along, boy." But when she wasn't looking, Oscar reached into the basket, grabbed a stem and tossed a breadfruit into the bush at the side of the road. He repeated this as often as he could. Only half the number of breadfruits he started out with in his basket made it to Cattlewash that day. When she discovered his trickery, Clotilda picked up a piece of drift wood and started to beat him. He ran away, only to get the rest of his licks when he sneaked into the house that night.

The sale of breadfruits eventually became Oscar's principal source of income and Bathsheba was the perfect location for this line of work. Breadfruits were bountiful in Bathsheba, more so than anywhere else in Barbados. On a walk through the village, you couldn't help but notice them. Green balls surrounded by large green fan-shaped leaves and a coot sticking out next to the breadfruit, even more phallic in appearance when between a pair of breadfruits.

Boys from Bathsheba, when they first went to school in Bridgetown, were often teased by being asked, "Is true that a boy born in Bathsheba is eat breadfruit for breakfast, brunch and brinner?" Breadfruits in Bathsheba were eaten in a great variety of ways, but you hadn't lived in Bathsheba until you had eaten roasted breadfruit on the beach on a moonlit night. You sliced a piece off the top, scooped out the heart and filled the cavity with salt beef and butter then roasted it over an open fire. Before you ate a piece, you dipped it into the sea to cool it down and add to the salty flavour.

In Bathsheba, locals didn't buy breadfruits. Those without breadfruit trees were never refused if they asked. Bathshebans sold breadfruits to restaurants and hotels in and out of the area and to markets in Bridgetown, too. They were a tradable commodity even for unemployed persons or down-and-outs who bartered them outside of the village. Such persons were called *breadfruit-swoppers*, a term which made its way into the Barbados lexicon to describe any person on the breadline and scratching for a living.

During the Second World War, when commercial shipping into the island virtually ceased, breadfruit trees produced more fruit than ever. So much so that they were called manna or god-fruits. Breadfruits ensured that Bathshebans never went hungry, and became part of the spiritual lore of the community. You cut the stem of a breadfruit and you would see a natural formation in the shape of the letter C. Every Bathsheban knew the significance of this. "Cain killed Abel under a breadfruit tree." They believed that the breadfruit tree witnessed the world's first murder and carried the letter C as evidence of Cain's guilt for ever and ever.

かしの

Everyone hailed Oscar as he pushed his box-cart of breadfruits through the village: the boys playing cricket on a little patch of pasture with a young breadfruit as a ball, the little girl pulling a breadfruit along the ground by a string tied to its stem, the men in Pops' rum-shop. Some, mostly the older ones, called out, "Oscar," and others, mostly the younger ones, "Oxcart." But you weren't always sure which they were saying.

His gaunt appearance belied a certain physical strength which enabled him to push his cart full of breadfruits uphill to the entrance of the hotel, where he often sold his produce. He wore a pair of old slippers on his feet, stained and ragged clothes, and a beehive of a faded tam to hold in his dreadlocks.

As Oscar approached the hotel, Aubrey Benskin's van overtook him. When Oscar arrived at the delivery entrance, Aubrey was already halfway through unloading his sweet potatoes, yams and bananas. His sinewy physique shifted the bags with ease.

Aubrey was a small farmer but larger than other farmers in and around Bathsheba. He had been a farmer all his adult life. He sold his sweet potatoes, yams, eddoes, cassava, christophenes, string beans, bananas, plantains and breadfruits to the few nearby hotels and restaurants and to hawkers who sold them in Bridgetown's markets.

Aubrey greeted Oscar with a polite, "Morning, Oscar."

Oscar replied with a perfunctory "Morning" and directed his gaze away from Aubrey.

"You got a lot of breadfruits there this morning," said Aubrey.

Oscar ignored Aubrey's attempt at conversation. They said nothing else to each other and proceeded to go about their business with the hotel. Business completed, each made his separate way back through the village, Oscar pushing his empty box- cart and Aubrey speeding away in his open-back Toyota van to his next delivery.

Oscar arrived home at his mother's chattel house and parked his box-cart in the back yard. He entered the back door of the sparsely furnished home. His mother was in the kitchen. "Here, this is for you, Ma," he said, handing her a $20.00 note, half of his morning's takings.

"You want a cuppa tea?" she asked. "Delores next door give me two piece of cassava and I bake some pone." The *two* was a mere figure of speech as she had been given several pieces of cassava. Oscar sat on one of the two chairs at the small unpainted wooden dining table with his tea and slice of cassava pone.

He looked out the window just in time to see Aubrey's van glide past. Aubrey lived in an old wall-house about three hundred metres uphill from Oscar and his mother.

ൟൟ

That afternoon, Aubrey walked into the mini-mart at the top of the village and saw Calvin Bourne, fellow small farmer, local preacher, neighbour and friend. Calvin loved the land and he loved his God. Aubrey was a younger man than Calvin. Aubrey's father, a farmer and *spekalater*—he bought and sold farm animals—had been a good friend of Calvin's. Aubrey farmed the four acres left to him by his father, just outside the village next to Calvin's piece of land. He lived four houses away from Calvin in the house in which he and his sister grew up as their father's only inside children.

"What's happening, Calvin?"

"Things slow, Aubrey, real slow."

"They say this going be a long recession."

"People getting lay off, people losing their jobs," said Calvin.

"Somebody thief some of my breadfruits from the tree near the road last night," said Aubrey, "and Germonica next door to me lost a bunch of bananas last week. I hear Miss Hessie barking last night but I ain't pay she no mind, thinking nobody would be foolish enough to climb over my fence. I still don't know how they did it."

"I losing breadfruits, too," said Calvin. "I don't mind a fellow taking a breadfruit to eat if he can't do no better, you understand, but stealing a dozen to sell is another matter altogether."

Aubrey looked around the shop, lowered his voice and said, "I feel it is Clotilda boy, the one that they used to call Crow, now they calling he Oxcart. She send he to high school and he learn good, got certificates, but he get in wid bad company. Start smoking dope, couldn't keep a job. He ain't too long come out of jail."

"You mekkin sport. Why, Clotilda got a little piece of land with two breadfruit trees and a few banana trees," said Calvin.

"Yes, but he got a friend in the market in town who taking whatever he can send. And he sending all the time even when Clotilda ain't got nothing on she trees. And he selling to hotels and restaurants in Bathsheba, too."

"I see he walking bout here like a poppet and people calling he a paro. But I din know that he is a thief."

"When these young people get hook pun the drugs, they will steal from their own mother to buy their stuff," said Aubrey.

"We should see if we can't hold him and call the police for him," said Calvin.

"Police? If I catch him on my land, it ain't no police in that."

"No, don't do anything foolish. Let we talk to his mother. She had enough bad luck already. We live like brother and sister for all these years in this village. I won't like to see the boy go back to jail again."

The two men continued their slow walk up and down the narrow aisles of the mini-mart, examining the shelves as they moved, but not putting anything in their baskets.

"I going have a word with Clotilda, she ain't too bright but I will make her understand that if it don't stop, we going hold the boy and call the police," said Calvin.

"Well, if I catch him on my ground, you going have to call the police for me," said Aubrey, raising his voice.

☙❧

Oscar sat on a coral stone block, once white but now weathered by time to greyish black, in his mother's backyard. The coral stone block was a discard, surplus to requirements for the propped foundations of their chattel house. With a metal file he sharpened the hook at the end of his breadfruit stick. The so-called stick was in fact a bamboo pole about twelve feet long. The hook was a rusted sickle which Oscar found in a grass-piece. He cleaned it up and strapped it with tightly wound wire to the end of the pole. Most people simply pushed a knife through the narrow end of a bamboo pole to pick breadfruits and removed it when they were finished. The sharpened sickle was Oscar's innovation. With the pole and his outstretched arms plus his five-foot, seven inches in height, he was able to reach way up in the breadfruit tree without having to leave the earth. His bit of maintenance completed, Oscar slid his breadfruit stick under the cellar of the house. As he straightened up, he became aware of being watched. He turned to see Calvin Bourne staring at him.

"Your mother home, Oscar?" asked Calvin, looking at Oscar through narrowed eyes.

Oscar nodded.

"Calvin, that is you?" Clotilda's voice called out from inside the house. "I here, bo, come in, nuh."

Calvin entered the back door, where he was met by the squat figure of Clotilda Greaves. Clotilda was still a powerful-looking woman with a thick neck, strong arms and a face that told of a life of hardship. Missing teeth made her cheeks appear as if she was sucking the marrow out of a bone. She and Calvin chatted for some minutes. Then Calvin said, "I come to talk to you about your boy. Breadfruits and bananas going missing in this village and people say it is Oscar that stealing them. They planning to hold him and call the police for him."

Clotilda clapped a hand to her forehead and closed her eyes. She shook her head from side to side, gritted what was left of her teeth, then opened her eyes. "Not my boy, Calvin. Not my boy. Just because he went to jail, he going get blame for everything now. The Lord know my boy don't thief. He let that wutless girl turn he foolish but he ain't no thief."

"I ain't accusing Oscar, I only telling you what people saying, you understand?"

Clotilda's mouth twisted from side to side. "You know how hard I work all my life. I head breadfruit up and down this place, I cut canes, I fork ground and I ain't got nothing to show for all my hard work. I send that boy to high school. He learn good, had a good job, then let some wutless girl addle he brain with dope. When he was in jail, I ain't had no body to help me. I got arthritis in these two hands, things hard with me now, Calvin. The little coconut bread and pudding and souse I sell pon a Saturday don't make much. I struggling to make ends meet."

Calvin saw the pain and desperation in her face. "Look, talk to the boy. Talk to the boy, you hear?" They were sitting across from each other at the small dining table. Calvin leaned forward, a concerned look on his face. "We work too hard to make a living out of the land. People getting vex. I come to warn you."

"I know who send you here, you know. He living up there in comfort. He supposed to be some kind o' family to Oscar father and he ain't even come to he cousin funeral. He say he was sick."

"Look, I got to go now." Calvin exited the back door to see Oscar walking away toward the two breadfruit trees in the far corner of the backyard.

࿙

That evening, Aubrey's wife, Mildred, answered the telephone. "Who is this? Who is this?" She hung up the phone, turned to a curious Aubrey and said, "Somebody say to tell you that they coming for some of your breadfruits tonight."

"Who, who say so?"

"I don't know, he sounded weird, like he had a towel over his mouth."

Aubrey steupsed. "Some foolish body ain't got nothing to do but make mischief."

His dismissal of the phone call the evening before did not stop Aubrey from walking outside the following morning to inspect his breadfruit trees. He was greeted by Miss Hessie, who had to have her morning cuddle before Aubrey was permitted to do anything else. Miss Hessie was a large mixed-breed, lion-coloured dog, with big drooping ears. Aubrey resumed his walk among the trees surrounding his house, Miss Hessie beside him. He stopped at a certain point and stared at the cut stem of a bunch of bananas that was there the evening before. He approached the banana tree, slowly put out his hand and caressed the stump of the stem. "I see why you were barking last night, Miss Hessie." He walked on, looking up at his breadfruit trees. He counted seven freshly cut stems. The caller had not been joking. If he was a mischief maker, he was a serious mischief maker. He looked around but noticed no sign of disturbance, no footprints. He got down on one knee and looked Miss Hessie in the eyes. "Did they drug you, girl?" Miss Hessie seemed perfectly fine. Aubrey walked back up the little hill to his house.

"Mildred, seven breadfruits and a bunch of bananas gone."

"You making sport, Aubrey."

"I ain't making sport and the body who phoned last night wasn't making none, neither. And I won't be making none if he come back again. I will be ready for him."

࿙

Oscar raised his breadfruit stick and positioned the sharpened sickle around the stem of a breadfruit. With a short tug, he severed the neck and the breadfruit fell into the bag. He had sewn half a crocus bag on to an old bicycle rim and had attached the rim at the cutting end of the breadfruit stick. This allowed a breadfruit when hooked, to drop directly into the bag rather than fall to ground and become bruised. He repeated this deft manoeuvre until he had enough breadfruits to fill his box-cart. He unhooked the bicycle rim, slid his pole under the cellar of the house and headed towards the hotel on the other side of the village where he regularly sold his breadfruits.

When he reached the point on the hill where it levelled off, Oscar saw a parked van. He recognized the van but thought nothing of it. Before he could overtake it, the driver's side door flung open and Aubrey jumped out. He pushed Oscar aside, grabbed the handle of the box-cart and tipped it over. The cart ended up lopsided in the gutter, its wheels spinning. Oscar was on his knees. He watched the breadfruits roll down the hill. Most settled in gutters on either side of the road but some kept on rolling all the way to the bottom of the hill. Oscar kept looking from the breadfruits to Aubrey, who was standing over him.

"You won't stop thiefing people breadfruits. If I ever catch you on my piece of property, you is a dead paro."

"Mr. Benskin, leave me alone." Oscar yelled in that flat tone of his that sounded as if his voice was blown through a pawpaw shank flute. "You got a fence 'round your place and a guard dog. Only somebody living at you could thief your breadfruits."

Four boys seated on a roadside bench at the bottom of the hill witnessed the assault from a distance. They ran to pick up the breadfruits. The tall one arrived first and helped Oscar to right the box-cart. He stuck his finger in Aubrey's face and said, "Benskin, why you don't leff the man?"

"Young boy, you think you can frighten me.? Well, let me tell you something, you play with fire, you get burn."

"Oh, yeah, you feel you is a gorrilliphant. Well, let *me* tell you something, fire will meet fire." The young man almost punctured his chest with his finger when he said "me."

The three other young men arrived with arms full of breadfruits. Aubrey turned and walked back to his van muttering to himself.

৯৶৶

The barking woke him up at 4:00 in the morning this time. Miss Hessie was barking herself hoarse. "Somebody got to be out there." Aubrey swung his legs off the bed and sat up. He was about to stand when Miss Hessie suddenly stopped barking.

"Where you going, Aubrey Benskin?" asked Mildred. "You ain't tell me that one of those wild boys threaten you yesterday? You willing to get kill for a few breadfruits?"

Aubrey got back into bed.

An hour and a half later he pushed open his back door. He made his way through the garden toward the breadfruit trees on the edge of his property. He saw the hind legs first, jutting out from a bush next to the fence. He hurried to her, sobbing as he went. He grabbed Miss Hessie's stiff legs and pulled her out of the bush. He dropped the lifeless legs. His head jerked backwards, he looked to the heavens with tightly closed eyes. "Oh, Gawd, oh Gawd," he bawled.

Germonica, in her nightgown, came running from next door. "What happen, Aubrey, what happen?"

His wife and their two teenaged boys rushed out of the house.

"Somebody cut off Miss Hessie head."

Germonica turned away, one hand over her eyes the other raised with an open palm and fingers stretched out. "But who would do such a thing, though, nuh?"

"Where is her head?" asked one of the boys.

"But you know, they like they carry way the head. It ain't nowhere bout here," said Aubrey. "They want war, well God blind them, they got war."

"Now listen to me, Aubrey Benskin, don't go and do anything foolish now," said Mildred.

"Don't talk to me, woman, talk to the body that start this. You and the boys can bury Miss Hessie."

Aubrey marched toward the house. Three passersby, villagers on their way to work, stopped and enquired what was going on. Aubrey burst out of his back door. He headed for the gate at the other side of the property, his father's old shotgun in his hand.

A woman shrieked and ran away. Mildred started to cry. Hands clasped on top of her head, she called out to her boys. "Stop wunnuh father, nuh." The oldest boy picked up a rock and ran after his father, the younger one followed suit. They marched with Aubrey across the road and down the hill to Clotilda's house, with an entourage of about six behind them, some yelling for blood, some pleading for peace, but no one really trying to stop Aubrey or his boys.

As Aubrey came around the side of Clotilda's house, Oscar dashed out and started running. He reached the banana patch. Aubrey started to raise the shotgun. The shotgun was halfway up when the sickle on the end of the bread-fruit stick encircled his neck, stopping him in his tracks. It jerked his head backwards; a little blood trickled down his neck on to his shirt.

"Drop the gun," shouted Clotilda, every vein and sinew in her thick neck standing out. "It is me you want, not my boy. You ain't going unfair him twice. Drop the gun or I will do you like I do your dog."

"Nyo, Ma, Nyo," yelled Oscar, squeezing the words out in his adenoidal tone.

An out of breath Calvin arrived, a bible in hand.

"Stop this madness," he yelled.

The shotgun fell from Aubrey's hands. The boys dropped their rocks. Calvin picked up the shotgun with his free hand. The bamboo pole with its blooded sickle dropped from Clotilda's hands and clattered to the ground. Clotilda fell to her knees.

Island Man

Bert Brathwaite stared at the email on his laptop monitor. It read, "Melanie Ruck wants to be your friend." His pulse quickened, his face lit up. The visceral reaction ended as soon as he noticed the return address on the unsolicited email. His smile turned to a frown. Just a social networking site trying to expand its membership through mined email addresses. Much to the irritation of his buddies, he stayed clear of social networking sites. They could be so time-consuming. He once suggested to his sister, Carmen, that she try adding up the amount of time she spent on Facebook. His close friends all had his email address, his home, work and mobile phone numbers. He didn't need Facebook.

He preferred to spend his spare time reading a good book. He ignored the message, tidied his desk and turned off his computer. But Melanie remained on his mind in the way that first loves always do. Where was she now, what was she doing? What did she look like, was she married, with kids?

About three months later, Bert was at his desk one afternoon when the phone rang. He picked it up and said, "Braffit." He always used the Bajan pronunciation of his name. There was a giggle at the other end of the phone. It was a giggle he hadn't heard for almost twenty years but one he would recognize if he hadn't heard it for forty or more.

తా✧

The bus beat Bert to the bus stop and, as he approached, a slim, shapely figure alighted and started to walk in his direction. He watched her with fascination; hips shifted left and right in what seemed like a choreographed walk. The engineering part of his brain pondered on the mechanics of it all. Another part of his brain said, "Wow."

She wore a pair of calf-length white slacks and an orange blouse with a small, ruffled collar. A neat bag with a long strap, draped over her shoulder, bounced off her right hip. He saw the giggle before he heard it. That giggle brought back memories. The squinty eyes and dimples were still there, and her face looked like 18 or 19, not 30. But that walk was new. The chubby 12-year-old girl whose mother had taken her and her siblings to join their father in the USA had returned as a very striking woman.

"Look at you," Melanie said and threw her arms around his neck. "Oh, Bertie, you look great, still as handsome as ever, even with that circle of hair around your mouth. Oh, I like the bald head, it suits you." She kissed his cheek and they clung to each other on the side of the road. He liked her smell. The raised soles of her wedge sandals brought her to within a couple inches of his five-foot-ten. They separated and looked at each other. Her cheeks were no longer plump enough to pull and her slightly overlapping front teeth were now perfectly straight. Her braided hair reminded him of the photo of the editor of the *Essence* magazines his sister was always reading.

"I couldn't believe it when I heard your voice on the phone. Why didn't you let me know you were coming?" Bert asked.

"I wanted to surprise you."

"Well, you certainly did. How did you find me, how did you know I would be here?"

"Ah, that would be telling, now."

There was something that hadn't changed her penchant for the arcane.

He took her hand and guided her over the well-worn pathway down to the beach. They picked their way through driftwood, washed-up bits of coral and picnic refuse. Once on clear sand she removed her sandals as they searched for their spot where a seagrape tree used to be. It is what she wanted to do. She had said, "No, don't pick me up at my uncle's house; I want to meet you in Bathsheba and I want to take the bus just like I did before. The church excursion to Bathsheba the day before I left was the last time we saw each other."

They found their place on the sand, stood there looking at each other. He smiled, she giggled. They looked out over the ocean. She had chosen a perfect Bathsheba day. A light breeze coming off the Atlantic took the edge off a big yellow sun staring out of a clear blue sky. White caps bounced and rolled toward them with a gentle roar, splashing and lapping the seashore. She put an arm around his waist and he put an arm around her shoulder.

"Why didn't you come to the airport?" she asked.

Bert hesitated, thinking how immature he had been. "I couldn't bear to watch you go. I thought you would be gone forever, that I was losing you to America."

He didn't mind sitting on the sand in his working pants but she couldn't be persuaded. "You should really have brought a towel," she said.

They left their place on the sand and walked hand in hand, along the beach at first, and then she slipped on her sandals as they moved onto the old train track in the direction of Cattlewash. "Someone just waved at us," she said. He turned but the car had already sped by.

"Did you get the number?" he asked.

She threw her head back, laughed and said, "I am back in Barbados for sure."

"How is your family?" he asked.

She had a baby brother, born ten months after they arrived in the USA. Her two younger sisters were both well and married with children. "Me, married? Hah. They tell me I'm too difficult to please." Her mother was anxious to see her settle down and have some children but told her many times that she kept choosing the wrong man.

"My mother was so excited when I told her you were in Barbados," Bert said. He didn't tell her that his sister had been noticeably nonchalant.

"What's your girlfriend like?" Melanie asked, looking straight ahead.

Bert stopped walking. "How did you know I have a girlfriend?"

She turned her face to him and said with a smirk, "You would be surprised to hear what I know about you. But you haven't answered my question."

"Clearly, I don't need to. You know everything. Don't you?"

They both laughed and walked on. Bert looked straight ahead at the long curve of the bay, past Belleplaine and out to Pico Tenerife. "She is wonderful," he said. He wasn't sure why he lied. He kept looking as far in the distance as he could. He was never a good liar. He and Vonda had separated quietly a month ago even though she still called him every day.

"Let's go up to the bar on the hill."

He quickened his pace, dragging her up the sharp incline and up the steps to the bar and restaurant perched on a mound at the lower end of the steep hill. She giggled. "If I did not have on these silly shoes, I would outrun you."

They arrived on the patio, panting and laughing. They walked toward the entrance, but she tugged at his arm and said, "Let's sit outside."

They turned, headed for an outside table overlooking the ocean and dropped into two chairs. He ordered a Banks. She wanted a beer, too, but changed her mind. Instead she pointed to a glass on a nearby table and said,

"I'll have one of those." A big-bottomed waitress with a big smile, a gold tooth and some Asian woman's hair on her head brought them their drinks and lunch menus. Melanie's drink was a fruit punch with a slice of pineapple that had started its life somewhere in Central America, a Maraschino cherry from Canada and a Chinese paper parasol on the rim of the glass that was made in America.

"Did you enjoy growing up in America?" Bert asked. Ahead of her peers at school when she first arrived in America, she went to college on a scholarship, then to New York for her MBA. In New York, she lived with a rich uncle in Brooklyn. "I have to tell you about him sometime. He lived the American dream," she said.

"But in college I worked as a bartender, got incredible tips. I also did some modelling. Both paid for everything else I wanted during my student years." She now worked as a vice-president in charge of marketing for Massachusetts Beer Works, a Boston microbrewery. "Everyone calls us Mass Beer." She had met the boss of the brewery while bartending and impressed him with her knowledge, her skills. "And most of all my enthusiasm and intelligence," she said matter-of-factly, without, thought Bert, sounding arrogant. Six months ago she broke up with her boyfriend of two and a half years. She had not dated since. It was her mother's idea that she should take a trip to Barbados. She was unconvinced because she had been away for eighteen years and had lost touch with old friends. But her mom told her that she could never be lonely in Barbados.

"The longer mom stayed away from Barbados, the more idyllic she made it sound."

They ordered flying fish sandwiches. They teased each other about their accents, his dry Bajan drawl and her Bostonian, stretching syllables till the elastic in them almost popped and with an occasional unmistakable dash of Bajan.

He started to tell her how happy he was with his engineering career. She interrupted, gently reaching over to put a hand on his, to say, "Have you any idea what engineers earn in the US? I am sure it must be at least double what you are getting here."

Bert was pensive for a moment then said, "I could probably earn four times as much in Dubai, but would I want to live there?"

She sat back in her chair, looked out to sea, twirled a finger around the tip of one of her braids. "I am really looking forward to this week. I hope you can find some time to take me around."

After lunch, they walked along the road toward Pops Bar, where Bert had left his car. They walked past little wooden holiday cottages painted in a variety of colours. Melanie thought the entire area needed landscaping, "to bring a sense of order and added beauty to the location." When they reached his car, one of the boys sitting in the gallery outside Pops whistled and called out, "Angel, when you go back up to heaven put in a good word for me, nuh?"

"I will," she replied with a hearty laugh and a wave in his direction.

"Why did you answer him?"

"Because he said something nice. You should hear some of the things I have to put up with when I walk down some streets in Boston or through Copley Square."

She asked if it was OK to turn off his car radio so that they could talk. He said it was. He ignored the dull ring tones of his Blackberry as he drove her slowly back to her uncle's house in St. Peter. As the car stopped, she leaned over and kissed him gently on the lips. "I really enjoyed the afternoon. I will see you tomorrow night, then," she said. "You choose the restaurant, my treat."

"I will call you in the morning."

"You had better, buster," she said with a mock threatening look, followed by a giggle as she opened the car door.

Outside the car, she turned, lowered her head and looked through the window, smiled and blew a kiss. As he drove off he glanced at his rear view mirror and saw her still standing there, watching him until he turned out of the gap. He thought he heard a giggle. On his way home her fragrance stayed with him and each time he recalled her gentle kiss, a warm shiver ran through his body. The little girl whose family took her away and whose two letters he never replied to had come back to him. The hand of fate, his mother would call it.

At home, he emailed his boss and requested four days off after the following day. He messaged his buddies, the rest of the so-called quintet, a group of old school friends, to tell them he would be out of circulation for a week. He asked Ezra, the member of the group closest to him, to take his place as referee for the kids' football game that Saturday afternoon. The replies came back swiftly. "Whuh gine on Dog? Whuh gine on bro? Whuh gine on?"

"Ah, that would be telling," he messaged back, smiling with each press of his thumb.

இ௸

"Why you don't return my calls? Who is the woman you were down Bath-sheba with today?" Two questions, or more, at once were typical Vonda. Bert was used to it so didn't answer right away. Months ago she repeated her condition that he had to put an engagement ring on her finger if he wanted their relationship to continue. It was the third time she had brought it up. The first time was an afternoon right after they had made love. "So when are you going to put a ring on my finger?" The second time was as he tried to get cosy while watching a movie at home. "It is about time we got engaged, Bert Braffitt." The third time it was an ultimatum, issued one evening after he had picked her up from work to go fetch her car from the mechanic. "We have been going out for two years, now. If we don't get engaged in the next three months, this is over, o-v-e-r."

Bert had every intention of telling her about Melanie but in his own time. Now she had turned up at his apartment as if she forgot that they agreed to go their separate ways. "Damn cell phones, damn life in a small island," he said to himself. He looked at the woman who had mesmerised him when they first met. The woman who said that she was attracted to him because, "you are not like the other men. I never hear you at football talking 'bout all the women you foop." Vonda, the woman of many hairstyles; today, her head adorned with a crown of lightly twisted tufts. She was pretty, even with her fleshy lips pouted. She was short and feisty with a round face, a determined countenance. He shook his head.

"Let me ask you again Bert Braffit. Who was the woman you were down Bathsheba with today?"

"That was Melanie Ruck, visiting from Boston. It's her first time back since she left Barbados eighteen years ago. We met for a drink and some old talk."

"Was she your girlfriend?"

"Yes. Well, kids stuff. You know. We were twelve years old when they emigrated."

"How come you never told me about her before? Why didn't you tell me she was here? How long is she here for? Why are you so damn secretive?"

"Which question do you want me to answer first, Torqs?"

"Please don't call me by that name," Vonda snapped. "I am *not* bloody Torquemada. Whenever you don't want to answer a question, you start with your sarcasm. Are you seeing this woman again?"

"I hope so. I wouldn't like her to leave without seeing her again."

Vonda pouted, turned her head and looked out the window. "Look, just be honest with me. Have we a future together, Bert?"

"Not if you never miss an opportunity to criticize me," Bert replied, looking out of the window with her. "Too besides, our compatibility issues may be insurmountable." It was an effort for him to say those words. Not because he didn't mean them—he certainly did—but he was never comfortable saying harsh words to anyone.

"It's because of this girl, isn't it? Well, I am out of here and out of your life, Bert Braffit."

ȣȣ

"Have you booked a restaurant?" Melanie asked when Bert called the next morning. Her cheerful voice brought a broad smile to his face and a glow of warmth to his body.

"Not yet. But that's OK. I'll pick you up at 7:30."

That evening Bert pulled up in front of the steps to Melanie's uncle's house. Melanie waved from the window and headed for the door. Her backless stilettos made clacking sounds as she tripped lightly down the fifteen front steps of her uncle's house perched on the side of a hill.

She wore a short tight sequined black top, the spaghetti straps superfluous for support. The top ended above her navel and her designer jeans were low-cut, exposing a band of flawless black flesh.

She turned off his car radio as soon she sat in the car. She said she had visited Speightstown that morning, spent some time in the museum and the Gallery of Caribbean Art. "There's some good work there. Have you been?" No, he hadn't. He preferred photography to modern paintings.

They headed down the west coast through Holetown. Melanie asked questions all the way. "Who lives in these luxurious villas behind those big gates? Where do people move to when they convert their houses into bars, restaurants or shops? Why are there still so few sidewalks?" She wanted an explanation for her every observation.

They drove through Paynes Bay and on to Derricks in St. James, where Bert took the car around the back of the Cariba restaurant, a converted chattel house, and parked on the grass. As Melanie turned to get out of the car he caught sight of part of a tantalizing tattoo in the small of her back.

"We don't have a sea view," Melanie lamented as they walked toward the entrance.

"Well, you did say the choice was mine," replied Bert. "This restaurant might be on the wrong side of the road, but the food is always good here and I like the relaxed atmosphere and unpretentious service."

They were welcomed warmly by the chef-owner, Glenn. "What's happening?" he asked and extended a fist to Bert for a bump. He quickly turned to Melanie and bowed, "good evening, my dear." He led them through the extension on the western side to the lower garden section of the restaurant and seated them in the far corner next to the tall croton hedge, which partially blocked out the house next door. He handed them over to a waitress and dashed back to the kitchen.

"What beers do you have?" Melanie immediately asked. "What, no American beers?"

"Did you come all this way just to have what you left at home?" Bert asked.

"Point taken." She giggled. "I'll have a Banks, then."

When the beer arrived she held it up to the light, admired its sparkle and its light straw colour. She put the glass to her nose and inhaled. "Hmmm, vibrant smell, a hint of citrus." She took a sip and proclaimed it, "Zesty, not bad at all. Could be crisper, though."

Bert studied her face as she went through her ritual. Looking at the refracted image of her nose through the beer glass he finally understood what was different about her face. "Your nose looks different," he said.

"You are incredibly observant, you know. I've had some minor aesthetic modification," she responded in her Bostonian accent, and with the wave of a hand, as if she was shooing away a fly. "Nuhbigting," she added in an exaggerated Bajan accent.

Bert smiled.

"You still aren't much of a talker, are you? But I know what you are thinking. No. Nothing else, nowhere else."

Bert chuckled. "Tell me something. Does an aesthetic modifier charge more than a plastic surgeon?"

"You haven't lost your sense of humour, either, Bert Brathwaite. But there are plastic surgeons and then there are plastic surgeons. I suppose you could say the same about engineers."

She smiled and giggled a lot during dinner. But there was a hard edge, a certainty about her when she discussed certain topics. Melanie often spoke her opinions as facts. "If you work hard in America, you will succeed. Dad held down two jobs from the time he arrived. He spent his first two years in Brooklyn, working for his uncle Ebenezer, his sponsor, before moving to Boston. He was an electrician by day and drove a gypsy cab at night and later a limousine, seven days a week. By the time he sent for us, five years later, he had bought a house. It was a fixer-upper, and he and his building buddies did an amazing conversion job on it. One day, I'll show you the before-photos."

She thought that women would run the world in less than two generations. "More women are going to college, outperforming men. More women are going into law. Our congress and senate, and parliaments around the world, are full of lawyers. It's only a matter of time." All said with an air of confidence that, Bert felt, must be taught in every American school.

The waitress arrived and placed his jerked pork chop with sweet potato fries and her special of pan-seared grouper with grilled christophene and basil-infused plantain croquettes in front of them.

"Did you like Trinidad?"

"Jesus, woman, who sent you my resume? No, don't tell me. It was my sister, wasn't it?"

"Now, now. That would be telling," she said, laughing.

"I am serious," he said.

"It's a small world now, Bert."

"I loved Trinidad. I stayed on and worked for a year after university. A very creative place, with very creative people, and Trinis know how to party. But I wouldn't like to live there, to raise a family there. Too much crime."

Bert paused then wanting to turn the attention to Melanie, asked, "why did you break up with your last boyfriend?" .

"He didn't seem to enjoy my success," Melanie said. She thought she had found *The One* but things started to fall apart after her last promotion at work. She didn't know if it was because she now earned more than he did. He changed, became moody, insisted on picking up the tab whenever they went out. One night his credit card was declined and she paid the bill. He sulked for the rest of the evening. They quarrelled. He said silly things about Caribbean people, "accused us of acting superior to African-Americans."

71

"Would you believe that some noted African-American scholars would like the US government to exclude Caribbean people from affirmative action stats? They claim we come from wealthy families and have had special education opportunities."

"That's unbelievable," said Bert. "I want to tell you one of the things I like about living in Barbados. One day I was in the supermarket and ran into our Prime Minister pushing a shopping cart, all by himself. No security and no one bothering him. I like that."

Melanie nodded slowly and Bert saw the concern on her face. "If Obama's elected, he'll need *extra* security, not less."

"You really think he can win?"

"Certainly. The cynic in me says that the Republicans don't want it. The economy is in too bad shape. Hey, let's talk about the rest of the week," she said and withdrew a list from her handbag.

She asked the waiter to slow things down. They were the last to leave the restaurant.

After dinner, Bert suggested coffee back at his little apartment under his parents' home. She said it was too late. Her uncle would be waiting up for her. "He thinks his sister's daughter is still a little girl."

The gentle kiss was longer this time when they arrived at her uncle's house.

༺☙

Bert lay in bed, thoughts racing through his head. She seemed so different to what he expected. That combination of confidence and charm was captivating. Sleep escaped him until the early hours of the morning.

First thing next morning Bert called Ezra. Ezra, the worldly one who always laughed at Bert's innocence. Bert wanted to find out where he could take *the test,* discretely. The night before, Melanie had severely criticised women who had sex with men whose HIV status they didn't know. She had agreed with him about the importance of trust in a relationship, but, she said, sounding rather Oprah-like, "You only trust instinctively in an emergency, and you don't have emergency sex."

"The bad news, buddy, is that you won't get the results for a week," Ezra warned him.

They put her activities list into action from the following day. He walked up the steps to meet her uncle before they set off and survived a grilling. "Who were his parents? Where did they come from? Where did he work?" The old man seemed satisfied that he could entrust his sister's daughter to the care of this young man and managed a friendly farewell, "have a good day, you hear."

"I answered those same questions two or three times already," said Melanie, as they made their way down the steps.

They picnicked on the beach at Bathsheba where she picked out her dream house, a purple-heart cottage with a veranda, near to Pop's Rum Shop. They took a leisurely walk through Andromeda Gardens and joked about their tentative steps at young romance, from quick, little glances and coy smiles to nervous, uncertain first words. They bought coconut water from a road-side vendor and she drank it like she had never before tasted coconut water. They paid a visit to Banks Breweries, where Bert had arranged a meeting with a member of the management team, a friend of a friend, for a tour of the establishment.

Melanie wanted beach time and Bert picked a couple of beaches he thought she would like, and she did. She was pleased at some of the physical developments in Barbados but was appalled at what she considered the copying of some of the worst elements of American culture. She swore the first few times she saw young men with their pants halfway down their backsides. "Do they know that's a prison style?" she asked. After that she steupsed or smirked and rolled her eyes.

On Sunday he invited her to lunch with his mum, dad and Carmen on Whitehall main road. His family had moved there when he was five years old. His parents had chosen a house with a grand view from its back patio, with Grazettes in the foreground and the Bridgetown harbour in the distance. From there they could watch all the cruise ships slipping in and out of the harbour. The house was built on a slope with an apartment under the back patio. Bert moved into the apartment a little after he returned from Trinidad.

Coral Brathwaite scanned Melanie from head to toe the moment she walked through the door. "My, my, you are so beautiful. I love this African print halter dress and that gold brocade is stunning." Bruce Braithwaite put his glass down on the sideboard, his eyes lit up and he gave her one of his bear hugs. Carmen's greeting was demure but soon she and Melanie whispered and giggled a lot.

"Your mother killed the fatted calf," his dad said, laughing heartily. Melanie enjoyed it all, the roast pork and flying fish, and ate almost half of a cassava pone, one slice at a time, revelling in the nostalgic flavour.

Melanie was off the next day. Bert made it to the Grantley Adams airport this time. After check-in, they walked over to Chefette, bought two rotis, a mauby for her and a chocolate milk-shake for him. Clinging to each other at the entrance to the departure lounge, they promised to be together soon again, either in Boston, Barbados or somewhere else. She boarded at the last possible minute, wiping her eyes yet smiling, waving, and looking back until she was out of sight.

He climbed the stairs to the viewing area and watched her until she disappeared into the aircraft. Bert drove slowly on the way home, Melanie on his mind. He could hear her giggle, see her aesthetically modified nose and he tried to imagine what the rest of that tattoo looked like.

He shook his head at the thought of a long-distance relationship. He recalled the story of a student at St. Augustine who wrote home to break off his relationship with the girl he left behind. He wrote that he had fallen in love with someone else. "What does she have that I don't have?" was her swift response. "Nothing, but it is here," was his reply.

৯৵৻

Bert pulled his car into his driveway, turned off the ignition, picked up his blackberry and checked his messages.

"You gone through the eddoes, dawg."

"You didn't even let the men get a glimpse."

"Welcome back, bro, I thought we lost you."

"I don't believe she is as beautiful as you say, man."

He messaged back, "meet me at Benskin's bar this evening. I have pictures."

৯৵৻

Vonda kept calling, too. After their fourth phone conversation, it struck him that he had managed to speak with her for over an hour and a half without any show of anger or complaint about something or other on her part. Where did that anger come from? Vonda had excelled academically at school; she was always near the top of her class. She had overcome all the classic indicators of a disadvantaged upbringing. The oldest of five children raised in a government housing-scheme by a single-mother, she helped to parent her younger siblings. He thought of those girls and women he saw walking along Broad Street on mornings when he was on his way to work. Dressed in smart suits, high heels, hair beautifully styled, and wearing that don't-mess-with-me look on their made-up faces. Where did that come from? His grandmother had that look but she lived in a different Barbados, she lived in real hard times.

Bert grew to enjoy his conversations with Vonda. He wondered how long she could maintain the effort. When he declined her invitation to dinner for old times' sake, she stopped calling.

ॐॐ

Their Blackberries buzzed daily and Bert installed a Magic Jack. He sometimes preferred it to Skype. At least it was still a telephone. Of course, with Skype they could see each other. He and Melanie planned a short break in New York at the end of November, bridging their national holidays, Barbados Independence and American Thanksgiving. Bert had recently acquired a new passport but had not yet renewed his US visa. There was a tedious online process to make an appointment for an interview at the embassy and it took three efforts before he got everything right. The appointment did not obviate the need for queuing outside the embassy. In the queue, he heard not only Bajan but multifarious Caribbean accents including French Patois, a reminder that the US embassy in Barbados also served the Eastern Caribbean.

Once inside, he found a seat next to a woman from Dominica. She was with her son and daughter. She said they were planning a trip to Disney World. They had flown in the night before and stayed in a guesthouse outside of Bridgetown. They were soon called and Bert moved to the end of his row nearer to the interviewing officer. The officer, a fresh faced young man with a crew cut, wanted to know how the Dominican lady would pay for her trip. She pulled out a bankbook and passed it to him. He jerked his head backward, blinked a couple of times and raised his eyebrows.

"Dominica is a very poor country. How did you come by this money?" asked the officer.

The woman raised her voice. "Eh, eh, I work for my money, young man."

"I'll be right back," said the young man. He slid off his stool and left his post. Bert could see him talking to a pink-faced man with wavy white hair and a neatly trimmed white moustache. The Dominican lady turned and said to no one in particular, "What he tink? He tink I dis ho?

Sa mère est la jammette!" Her son looked around and when he saw that Bert was paying attention put a hand over his eyes. Bert started to estimate the cost of the woman's trip to Barbados, flights and accommodation for her and the children plus the application fee, the latter a week's pay for many islanders. If she failed to get the visas for her and the children, that money would be lost. The white haired-man patted the shoulder of the young officer who returned to his post, stamped vacation visas in the three passports and handed them back without a word. The Dominican lady smiled and said, "God bless you, son," and rolled her eyes as she turned away.

Bert's officer was a middle-aged man. He chatted with Bert as they went through the process. He asked Bert about his favourite NBA team. Bert was more of a football-man but would watch the basketball finals with his buddies.

In the middle of the conversation, the officer remarked, "You know, engineers earn pretty good money in the US." The night before, Ezra had been telling the guys the story of his driving test. "Take the next right," the examiner casually directed him during the road test. The next right would have taken Ezra the wrong way down a one-way street. "We don't do too badly in Barbados, you know," Bert replied. He left the embassy after about two hours. As he left he noticed that the queue was just as long as when he arrived. It seemed like everyone wanted to go to America.

আ≪

Bert flew out to New York on the 26ᵗʰ of November. It was a Wednesday, the day before American Thanksgiving. He had taken a week out of the following year's holiday, having already used up all his days for 2008. The following Monday was a holiday in Barbados, Independence Day, which fell on the Sunday.

. "So, you giving up your independence for this woman?" asked Ezra when Bert came over to borrow his brown leather jacket with the furry inside. That jacket had served Ezra well during his college days in New York.

"And she is giving thanks," replied Bert. "This year's Thanksgiving is extra special because of the Obama election."

. "I am anxious to talk to you when you come back, man. In fact, I am sorry I am not coming with you, just to get a feel of the post-election mood there. You will enjoy New York. And Harlem is going through something of an evolution, they call it gentrification. Bill Clinton has an office there now."

Then Bert said, "Melanie really wants me to come live in America."

Ezra pushed up his mouth, squeezed his lips together in a way that communicated his thoughts before he uttered them.

"I thought so. Get her to come here, man. America doesn't need you, or me. Barbados needs people like us, to keep it growing, to keep it going. America doesn't need Melanie, either, but it sounds like she needs America."

Bert didn't answer.

"Hey, man, have a good time. And don't forget your certificate, now," said Ezra, laughing as they hugged.

જ્જ

Melanie had accepted the use of an apartment of friends who would be out of town for the long Thanksgiving weekend.

"Don't come to Boston. I'll meet you in New York. I want you all to myself," she said, giggling.

Bert said he would take a cab from JFK to the apartment but Melanie insisted on meeting him. She shrieked his name and waved her hands wildly as he entered the arrivals hall. He lifted her off her feet and heads turned to watch them. They walked out arm in arm to a limousine driven by one of her father's old colleagues. She took off her beanie hat and shook out her straightened hair as they settled in the back of the limousine. Her lips met his in a long warm kiss.

The Studio apartment on Frederick Douglass Boulevard in Harlem was small; Bert estimated it was about five hundred square feet. In contrast to the chilly November air outside, it was comfortably warm inside. The light brown décor worked well with the dark brown trimmings and modern furnishings. A large rectangular glass window overlooked the boulevard and flooded the room with light during the day when the vertical blinds weren't drawn.

Melanie produced some cold cuts, a bottle of California sparkling wine and two champagne flutes. She set them on the coffee table and turned on the radio, already set to a station playing cool jazz music. Bert examined the label on the wine bottle. He chuckled and read the label out loud, "*Iron Horse Brut X Green Valley of Russian River Valley Sparkling Wine.*" He was intrigued by what he called, "this bit of intrinsically American naming." He opened the bottle with a small pop and filled the two flutes. They clinked glasses, sat on the sofa in front of the coffee table, snacked and sipped and hugged and whispered and laughed and kissed. They topped up their glasses, left the half-finished plates on the coffee table, the music playing, and retreated to the bedroom and deferred pleasures.

Bert traced a finger along the dark red ridges of Melanie's spinal tattoo. To him, it looked like some complex, oriental drawing. "It's a Chinese zodiac sign. The year of the horse. I had it done as a teenager," she said.

He loved the velvety texture of her skin and her soft, sweet gasps when he gently raked his lips over it.

"You called out Vonda's name when we were making love."

"Oh, God, I am sorry."

"It's alright, I understand."

He hadn't even realized and would not have known if she hadn't told him.

"You never once tried to seduce me in Barbados. I wasn't sure what to make of that. Why didn't you?"

"Ah, that would be telling."

. Melanie chuckled. She raised herself, rested on her elbows, breasts dangling on the rumpled sheet. She turned her head to look at Bert. "You know, I think I never stopped loving you. Perhaps that's the real reason that none of my relationships worked."

Perhaps the same applied to him, thought Bert. The mention of Vonda triggered memories, though. She was bright, brash and outspoken, but forthright and honest. If it weren't for her irascible nature, they would have been engaged by now, even though neither his mother nor sister was overly enthusiastic about her. His mother once said that Vonda made up for his shyness. "Too cocky, too crude." Carmen repeatedly said.

Bert had left the itinerary for the week up to Melanie. "Just include a bit of shopping, I need to get gifts for folks back home, but nothing before ten o'clock in the morning." Melanie reached over to the bedside table, slowly stuck two fingers in her handbag, extracted a single sheet of paper and waved it in front of Bert's face. She giggled. Bert looked over the itinerary and was relieved to see that it was not action-packed.

There were three planned dinners: Thanksgiving with uncle Ebbie in Brooklyn, one at Sylvia's, a place he had heard of, and the other at Aquavit, which he didn't think he knew at all, but when Melanie mentioned the owner's name, Marcus Samuelson, he recognised the celebrity Swedish-Ethiopian chef. There was a visit to the Schomburg, and the rest of the time was to be decided.

Bert didn't particularly want to do the Thanksgiving dinner. From what little he had heard from Melanie, Ebbie was a mean old coot. Melanie really wanted him to go.

"Somebody should write a book about this man," she said. Ebbie was really her great-uncle, her grandmother's brother. He had lived in the US since 1951. He had no more than a primary school education but was a Mr. Fix-it, a good mason, carpenter, plumber and so-so electrician, in Barbados. In Brooklyn, his skills became much sought after because he had earned a reputation for excellent work. The demand for his services was so high that he could eventually choose his clients, and charge above the average rate. At some point he bought a coin-operated laundromat. He kept the name on the outside, *Liberty Laundromat*, maintained the equipment and collected the money himself. Customers thought he was an employee and he never corrected them. Eventually he bought or established other laundromats and gave up working for other people. He then through his lawyer-client-friend Leonard Schwartz bought a foreclosed property at auction, renovated it and sold it for a tidy profit. He repeated this pattern; not just with foreclosures but any property on the market and in need of an upgrade. Leonard set up a holding company for Ebbie. Leonard's brother's real estate business handled all the purchases and sales.

Ebbie became rich. He had a son, Martin, who died in a car crash the year after he graduated from college. He drove head-on into a tree.

The coroner said that he may have fallen asleep at the wheel but there were rumours that it was a suicide, driven there by his father's too high expectations. Melanie's dad, his sister's son, was brought from Barbados to work for his uncle, even though Ebbie had a daughter, Florence, who was only two years younger than Martin. In a way, he was to replace Martin, but her dad and Uncle Ebbie never got on.

"The loss of his son drove him into a deep depression. Dad found him very difficult to work with, impatient and demanding. In addition, dad felt that he was not being properly compensated for his work. Uncle Ebbie always thought he was ungrateful. A friend from Barbados persuaded my dad to come to Boston and work with him in construction. Dad and Uncle Ebbie didn't speak for seven years after that."

Bert felt at ease in Harlem in spite of the warning of the doorman. "You got to watch *yoself* in this neighbourhood, buddy." He discovered Chill Berry's frozen yoghurts and a mobile restaurant that sold the meatiest frankfurter he had ever tasted. He liked the feel of the city, the skyscrapers, the smell of diverse foods everywhere and he quickly got used to the blaring of car horns. He was impressed by the attention of the staff in shops and remarked how friendly, articulate and confident everyone seemed. "Are Harlemites normally this friendly?" he asked.

"I think we are witnessing a bit of post-Obama election euphoria," Melanie said.

ৡৎ

"*C'est trop cher* ," said Bert, resorting to his schoolboy French when told the price of an attractive leather belt he wanted to buy from a *Senegalese* street vendor. The vendor's face lit up at the sound of French and the price came down. Didier soon corrected him on his nationality. He was from Côte d'Ivoire and his *camarade* was from Mali. "..*mais ici, nous sommes tous sénégalais.*"

He liked Harlem. For him, raised on a diet of American movies, it was like walking onto a film set. He enjoyed the beef short ribs at Sylvia's so much that he decided they should return for lunch. He thought the food at Aquavit was as good as Cariba's.

ৡৎ

. "Ain't no cabbie going take you to Brooklyn at night," said the doorman, responding to their enquiry. They resorted to the limousine driver and he returned to take them into Brooklyn for Thanksgiving dinner at Uncle Ebbie's. "We are here," the driver announced as he pulled up in front of a three- storey mansion on a tree-lined avenue in Brooklyn.

"I thought you said he lived on his own," said Bert as he got out of the limousine.

"He does. He just wouldn't move. He could go and live with his daughter out on Long Island but he didn't approve of her marriage, nor any of her previous suitors. She's a criminal lawyer and married to one of her former clients. I mean, he's not a street criminal, he is a college graduate, but he did a little time for a youthful indiscretion. Uncle Ebbie says she makes a living putting criminals back on the street. When she comes to see him, she isn't allowed to bring Johnny. Uncle Ebbie has a full-time caregiver, a Jamaican woman."

A short man with a natural tonsure an ancient monk would be proud of and a round brown face with dark patches under his eyes shuffled to the door a short time after the bell chimed. Melanie hugged him and he smiled a broad smile. He examined Bert from head to toe. "So you *is* the young man who going to marry my niece?"

"She hasn't asked me yet," replied Bert, smiling. Melanie blushed, then shook her head and laughed. Uncle Ebbie gave him a stern look.

The old man talked almost non-stop during the evening, in an American accent peppered with Bajan intonation and expression. The only sign of limited education was his occasional use of muddled grammar, the proverbial green verbs in Barbados. But there was no doubting his intelligence. He was up to date on world affairs, had followed the recent presidential election very closely. "I *sen*' Obama some money *troughout* his campaign, *yuh* know." He asked blessings for "our next President, my wonderful niece, and this young man from Barbados and for Ivy who prepared this wonderful dinner," in a long prayer before the meal.

He returned to Barbados only once, in 1969, for his mother's funeral. He heard that a lot had changed since his visit but he knew that if he had remained there, he would not have achieved what he had in America.

"When are you going to marry this girl?" he asked while Melanie stepped out of the room to help Ivy with the dessert. "You know, many of our smart young women have crossword options when it comes to marriage nowadays. You know what that is?" He searched Bert's puzzled face and saw he didn't have a clue. "They can go across or down," he said, motioning with a finger.

"He's an interesting man, your uncle," Bert said as they settled into the limousine on the way back to Harlem." I am glad I came."

Melanie smiled, snuggled up to him and closed her eyes.

ॐॐ

They walked to the *Schomburg Center* on Sunday morning. It was Independence Day back home in Barbados and the last day of the 'Aaron Douglas Exhibition', *Aspects of Negro Life*. They stood in front of *Song of the Towers*. Bert looked at it from bottom to top, side to side, over and over. Melanie drew close, put both arms around his waist and leaned her head against his shoulder.

"What are you thinking?" she asked.

"You are the art expert. What are you thinking?"

The painting was huge, 8 or 9 square feet. To Melanie, it depicted a vision of hope, freedom and joy. Bert thought there was a strong religious aspect to the painting. He compared the outward leaning of the skyscrapers, which revealed the Statue of Liberty in the distance, to the parting of the waters. There were three men in the picture. "Were they wise men following a star, or in this case circles of light, leading to the Statue of Liberty? Was the musician exulting because he had seen the Promised land?" But the musician was standing on the cogs of a giant wheel; that suggested, to Bert at least, that he would have to perform a perpetual balancing act to avoid being caught up in the machinery. He thought the figure on the left at the bottom of the painting, possibly the artist himself with his hand on his head, was another symbol of uncertainty.

"You are an eternal pessimist, Bert Braffit," Melanie said. "The machinery symbolises the transition for Blacks from an agricultural age to an industrial age. The musician is standing on the wheel of progress. He is going to blow that horn. Listen, man, let me take you to the Statue of Liberty. You cannot fail to be inspired by that."

They made it to the Statue of Liberty on Tuesday, the day before he returned to Barbados. Bert read the famous inscription. He kept staring at the words, his hands in his coat pockets, and Melanie slipped an arm through his.

"It's powerful, isn't it?"

"Where do I fit?" he asked.

"What do you mean?"

"Which of these boxes do I tick? I am not tired or hungry...well, poor is a relative term. Homeless or wretched refuse, thank God, no. And yes, I already breathe free."

"God, you can be so melodramatic," she said, shaking her head. "Come on, let's climb."

At the top and both out of breath, she leaned against Bert as they looked out over the city. "You have a point about the inscription, but everything has a context. To make it contemporary I would add one line: *bring me your talented.*"

"Hmm, that may have been a deliberate omission," said Bert, stroking his beard.

"I have a question for you. Do you know why you breathe free?"

"Why do you think I breathe free?" asked Bert, looking at her through squinted eyes.

"Because of this country. Yes, it's complex, but so is life. You don't have to tell me about its history of racism. I've lived here for eighteen years." She told him that her father didn't drive limos anymore but still had his chauffer's hat, which he kept in the family car. The staties..."

"The who?"

"That's Boston slang for state troopers; they didn't pull him over when he was wearing that hat."

She paused and looked out over the water. "In art class in high school some of the hoodsies started calling me six-c...."

"What's a hoodsie?"

"Oh, they are those too-fresh, young, teenage, Boston girls. At first I thought they were calling me sexy. They weren't. Six- c is the code for a pantone colour, black. But you know what? I have been called names in Barbados, too, because of the shade of my skin."

She faced Bert. "But I was asking *you*: Why do you think you breathe free? I want you to ask yourself how free you would be if the Nazis had won the Second World War."

"You know, America did not win that war by itself."

"True, but it would have been a different result without America, and we would've been set back two hundred years. We sure as hell would not be anointing a black US president next January. Come to think of it, I don't know if there would have been a black president anywhere on this earth."

"Hmm, you could be right," said Bert. "But I watch CNN and Fox and I see an expansion of extremist views. The vitriol is scary. Where's that leading? I can't deny America's place in history—its achievements are stellar—but it isn't just a complex country, I would add incredibly contradictory. Someone once asked, how do you fit the world's best universities, the most Nobel prize winners in the sciences and the Ku Klux Klan into the same box?"

"Freedom is freedom. You can't control it. You can't manage it," said Melanie.

പ്രൈ

They Skyped or messaged every day on his return to Barbados. They talked about a future together and disagreed as to where they would live. "Your engineering degree qualifies you for an H1-B visa and companies here are very keen on hiring foreign engineers. They like their work ethic."

A colleague from Bert's St. Augustine days had made that trip. He soon discovered that he was being paid less than his American counterparts. After six months, he brought it up with his employer and shortly after that lost his job and was deported.

The next day Melanie called to explain that if you applied for a Green Card, you would not be tied to a particular employer.

In early February, Melanie announced she would be back in Barbados for a few days. They had talked about her returning but not before Easter. Bert rushed to rent the house she had admired in Bathsheba. She flew in on a Thursday and left the following Tuesday. It rained intermittently over the weekend, unusual for the time of year. Clouds kept trying to smother the sunlight. It was a painter's sky, colours shifted from black to grey to orange to white with bits of blue peeking out from time to time. The rains brought mud down from Joe's River and dumped it into the sea. The tides carried it across the bay turning a swathe of the sea murky brown. Melanie enjoyed the veranda even during light showers but the wind gusts that occasionally doused the veranda forced them inside. Rain pounded the galvanized roof like tiny metal marbles, making them speak in loud whispers as they snuggled in bed. This time there was no sightseeing, it was bed, veranda, bed, beach, bed. When the sky cleared they managed a couple of power walks up Bathsheba's steep hills.

On Saturday they had a long lunch at the Village Bar in Lemon Arbor with the rest of the quintet, their wives and girlfriends.

As soon as they waved goodbye, Melanie spoke. "God, that was hilarious. Are they always that funny, or was it the rum? Do your friends always drink that much? And that Shernelle, Ezra's fiancée, she is so smart. Did you notice how she interrupted Ezra whenever he started to quiz me? But you know what was really good for me? To hang out with a group of fun-loving, intelligent, professional, young Bajans, I loved it. And that idyllic view of Bajan countryside. Wow."

ॐ✑

Sunday lunch was at Bert's beaming parents. Carmen called Melanie, "sis."

"I would like to retire here," Melanie said that evening as they sat on the veranda looking out over the Atlantic. "No more Boston winters. Instead, a wooden bungalow with a veranda in Bathsheba."

"Why wait until retirement? Why not come back here now?"

"Oh, Bert. Why don't you come up to Boston?"

There was a moment of silence before his delayed response. "Listen, I don't want to live in a country where a lunatic can walk into a store and buy a gun as easy as buying a loaf of bread."

"God, man, that's silly. You are making the mistake of judging a country by its worst elements," she said, passion rising in her voice. "Our children could go to some of the best schools in the world."

The "our children" surprised Bert. He hadn't thought that far yet. He frowned and looked away but said nothing.

"What's up now? Talk to me, man."

"I wouldn't want to raise my child in America," he said slowly and quietly.

"Oh, my God, why not?"

"You know, I've been to the US three times, and each time I have enjoyed it, particularly my last visit. I have never personally had a problem, but I cannot be blind or deaf to what I read and hear about what happens to other black people there. And if you think the election of a black president will change that over night, you are wrong. My suspicion is that his election will arouse lots of deep-seated animus."

"You are such a goddamned pessimist, man."

They had their first real argument. She said the statistics Bert trotted out wouldn't apply to people like them. "There are two Black Americas."

"Tell that to Ennis Cosby, whose father's fame or money couldn't protect him out on the street. Tell that to some under-educated cop with a gun who sees you out for an evening jog and decides that you don't belong in that neighbourhood that you have worked your tail off to buy into." Bert paused then added, "Think not of what you can achieve, but of who you are when you walk down the street."

The parody wasn't lost on Melanie and she was not amused by it. She sat up in bed and turned to face Bert, fire in her eyes then tears. Bert sat up and reached out to her. "Look, we will work this out," he whispered, "but please understand that I want to live here, to make my contribution to *my country*."

It was a short stay, much too short, but Melanie had to get back to work. She wept at the airport. Bert wanted to come up for Easter but she doubted she could get time off. "Easter is not a holiday in the US, you know." They postponed a decision on their next meeting. Summers were busy for Melanie. That's when America's beer consumption was at its highest.

જ∽⌒

Bert woke late. It was a Sunday morning. He walked up the steps at the side of his apartment and dropped his laundry in the basket next to the washing machine in the little laundry room at the back of the garage. He followed the aroma of his mother's cooking into the kitchen. He crept up behind his mother and kissed her neck. She turned and said with a smile, "Good morning, son. There is nothing to taste yet." Bert laughed, turned and walked into the living room. He flopped onto the old brown sofa, picked up the TV remote and, as he scrolled through the channels, called out to his mother, "Where is Carmen?"

"She went with her father, down to the gas station. They will be back soon."

He started to reach for one of Carmen's *Essence* magazines on the coffee table in front of him but her laptop was open to the left of it. He decided he would send an email to Melanie. He pulled the laptop around to face him and the screen lit up. It was open at Carmen's Facebook page.

Bert didn't hear the first time his mother asked if he wanted a cup of tea. The second time she asked, she had come into the room. He looked up to see her, wooden spoon in hand and a concerned look on her face. "Is something wrong, son?" He said that he was fine and he didn't need anything to drink. "I just looking at something interesting."

The something interesting was correspondence between Carmen and Melanie. Bert scrolled through the Facebook entries, seeking out the Carmen-Melanie exchanges. They went back several months.

"My brother is a technical man. If it can't be added, subtracted, multiplied or divided, he can't understand it."

"Maybe he has found the perfect partner, someone who adds zest to his life," replied Melanie.

"She adds more than zest. You should see her at football matches. She is part of the entertainment. She parades up and down the sidelines, yelling her head off, shouting abuse at some players and cheering others."

"Sometimes it is hard to believe that this Vonda has a degree. You know what they say…you can take it out of the housing scheme but…"

"She sounds earthy," replied Melanie…

Bert was still reading when he heard his dad's car pull up outside. The last entry he read was from Carmen. "Ghetto girl gone," it said. He quickly scrolled up to where he had started and shifted the laptop back to where he thought he had found it.

"I'll have that tea now, mom," he called out, rising from the sofa.

࿎࿎

The email from Melanie popped up while he was online one Saturday morning in May. The final paragraph read, "I am on a career path that I don't think I can duplicate in Barbados. To move to Barbados would be to put my career in reverse. I am being head hunted by a bigger brewery. It is out of state. I think I will accept. So, Island Man, wish me luck. I wish you well."

Why hadn't she called instead of writing, he wondered? But then, he felt the embers had been cooling about a month after her February visit to Barbados. He put it down to his unease about living and raising a family in the US.

He replied to the email, "Let's talk." He heard nothing in return. He messaged and phoned but she did not respond. He telephoned her parents home. Her mother said she was not there and that she would let her know he called. Was that tension in her mother's voice, or was he imagining things? Melanie never called back. His Blackberry messages went unanswered. He signed up to Facebook and tried to be a Facebook friend, but no response. He spoke to Carmen but she had not heard from Melanie. He called Mass Beer and left a message on her answering service. It was over, o-v-e-r, he told himself.

࿎࿎

"I'm really busy at work," Bert replied when Ezra called to find out why he hadn't heard him.

"Carmen tells me you are moping, man."

"No, man, I am on a big project. I'll be in touch soon."

He knew that Ezra was not convinced. Melanie was still constantly on his mind. Half a day's work now took him a day. He would stare at the AutoCAD drawings on his monitor for extended periods. He tried to rationalise his reaction to the situation, but couldn't.

He gave Vonda a call; just to see how she was, he told himself.

"I am fine, getting on with my life, thank you. And what has prompted this call, may I ask?"

He ignored the sarcasm in her tone and they chatted for a few minutes. He asked if she would like to have dinner with him, for old times' sake.

"You know, when you shoot for goal and the ball hits the cross-bar and rebounds, more often than not, someone else gets a chance to shoot," Vonda replied.

"You are talking in riddles. Is that a yes or no?"

After a pause she said, "That's a maybe, Bert Braffit."

He said he'd call again, and soon they were speaking regularly. She said yes the next time he invited her to dinner. Eighteen months later they married.

છ✧

Bert and Vonda moved into a rented house in West Terrace and settled into the life of a newly-married couple. They were saving hard to buy or build a house and talked increasingly often about starting a family.

One Saturday morning in March 2012, Bert had just returned home from refereeing a kids' football match. As he entered the door, the phone rang. He quickened his pace and picked up the cordless phone. It was Carmen and Bert couldn't tell whether it was excitement or panic in her voice.

"What's wrong with you, girl? Mom and dad all right?"

"Bert, you have to see this, Bert."

"See what? What are you talking about?"

"I am sending it to you as I speak."

"Sending what, Carmen?"

"She has resurfaced."

Bert rushed to his open lap top, on the dining room table. His fingers flew. His eyes settled on Carmen's email and he clicked on the link of the *Atlanta Caribbean News.*

The phone was on the table but he could hear Carmen yelling. "Have you opened it yet?"

Vonda appeared at his side in a long tee-shirt, the word UNITED emblazoned across her chest. She rested a hand on Bert's shoulder.   "What's going on, Bert?"

Bert didn't answer. His eyes were fixed on the page in front of him: *Women on the move* it read. Vonda leaned closer her arms around his chest.

Among the mini-bios of women making their mark in the business world was one accompanied by a sharp photograph of Melanie in a business suit and that look of posed confidence. The brief feature revealed that she was the new Vice-President of Peachtree Breweries in Atlanta. Bert gasped, open-mouthed.

"This can't end so," he blurted out.

Vonda leaned over, brought her arms up around his neck, her cheek pressed against his cheek.

"Yes it can," she whispered, "yes it can."

The final line in the article read: "The single mother lives in North Decatur with her daughter, Bathsheba, who celebrated her 2nd birthday last November."

Desmond, Lola and Bassman

It was during the early days of their courtship and their first time away together. They drove from London to Nottingham to attend a wedding. The bride was a Jamaican girl called Blossom, a friend of Lola's from their days at nursing college.

There was a live band at the reception (apparently a new band: no one at their table had ever heard of them) and there was nothing about their appearance to provoke any particular expectation. There was a tall, stringy, bearded, dreadlocked man, a bit older than the others, who seemed to be a roadie; he was doing most of the setting up. Desmond turned to Lola, "That chap looks more like someone you would expect to see swinging a machete on a banana plantation in Jamaica than lugging around musical instruments in Nottingham."

The band members disappeared while the wedding reception took its course and when it was their time to perform they returned in costume. A man at the table next to Desmond and Lola's asked loudly, "Zabandat?" Several people chuckled. A blond Englishman at their table asked, "Is Zabandat the name of the band?" There were more chuckles and the girl to Desmond's right translated the Jamaican for the Englishman: "He was being sarcastic. Is that a band? Is a band that? Zabandat?" Desmond smiled. He remembered his boyhood home, a regular meeting place for numerous Caribbean immigrants whose accents he learned to identify and understand from an early age.

The tall, bearded man, now wearing a colourful dashiki, made his way to the back of the bandstand and took hold of the double bass, which he had left leaning against the wall. He seemed to embrace the instrument for a moment then, while the other band members were getting their instruments ready, he proceeded to play, his head bowed, eyes firmly fixed on the floor. Desmond looked at the bass-man then around the room and back to the bass-man. The bass-man was playing *Sonnet in Search of a Moor,* a little known piece of Ellingtonia written with Billy Strayhorn for, and first performed at, the Stratford Ontario Shakespeare Festival back in the 1950s.

At the end of the introductory solo Desmond alone applauded. He did so with gusto and the bass-man jerked his head in his direction as if he had been prodded awake from an afternoon snooze. Their eyes stayed fixed on each other for a moment before the bass-man and Desmond exchanged knowing smiles, the performer appreciating the fan appreciating the performer.

The band started to play and the bass-man went to work. He leaned into the double bass, left and right hands uncoordinated to the eye but very coordinated to the ear. The left hand slid up and down the long neck of the bass, *sliding and holding, sliding and holding.* The right hand flew; fingers flailed, plucked, stroked, tickled and even slapped. His entire body moved continually and so did his mouth. He bit or pursed his lips, closed his eyes, stuck out his tongue, curled it to the left, curled it to the right.

People stopped talking and were looking at the bass-man, bodies moving in their seats. Some rushed to the dance floor and others approached the bandstand to watch and listen. It was a tight little band: sax, trumpet, keyboard, lead guitar, drummer and the bass-man. A singer joined them after a few pieces. But the bass-man was in a class by himself. He was the star of the show.

The crowd in front of the band grew. They applauded after each of the bass-man's decorative flurries and cheered at the end of every piece. A young man standing right in front of the bandstand turned to the other onlookers and declared, "Im better than Shakespeare." A few people looked at him with raised eyebrows and he said, "I mean Robbie, man, I mean Robbie." An Antiguan accent, belonging to a hugely pregnant lady, asked, "You tink he better than Family Man?" The question was answered with a long, "Chaah."

A tall, frail, elderly man, wearing a well-preserved old double-breasted suit and smoking a cigarette from a holder, asked Desmond in a rich Jamaican accent if he had ever heard of Lloyd Brevett. Desmond shook his head.

"This bass-man remind me of Brevett. He is the best bass-man I hear since Lloyd Brevett," said the old man, who went on to explain that Brevett was the bass-man of his day back home.

Desmond looked at the old man and said, "I never heard of Brevett but I hear Mingus, I hear Blanton, particularly Blanton in his playing. But tell me something, why isn't this man famous?" The elderly Jamaican tapped his right temple with his forefinger and then slowly shook his head from side to side and his eyes clouded over. "Very sad, very sad," he said.

The bass-man was sweating now in a room that was not hot. The band was having fun and so were the wedding guests. They danced and applauded and laughed and chatted with people they didn't know.

The band concluded its first session with an energetic short piece. The bass-man climaxed it, frenzied fingers flying to a crescendo, leaving his new-found fans to breathlessly bring themselves back to earth. There was loud applause and the other band members walked off the stage to pats on the back and high fives.

The bass-man stayed and commenced playing another solo. Bubbup… bubbup,,, bubbup…he played the same notes over and over. The room went quiet; people listened, exchanged curious glances, then smiles and laughter rippled through the room as they recognized a simple heartbeat. They became quiet again as they listened some more.

Bubbup…bubbup…bubbup…the heartbeats got slower and fainter until they disappeared. People remained quiet for a few moments then started to applaud. The applause was slow this time. There was a period of introspection and curiosity. Gradually the noise of conversation grew.

The bass-man leaned his instrument against the wall as gently as a mother laying her baby in a crib. Many of the wedding guests stood as the bass-man left the stage, a blank expression on his face.

He avoided eye contact as he made his way through the well-wishers, even with a very pretty girl who stood directly in his path. As he approached she adjusted the top of her dress to expose more bosom. "I am Joyce, I really dig your music, man, I think you great," she said in a delicate accent, which Desmond described as middle-class Grenadian. The bass-man nodded, walked around her, and exited into the cool September evening, dragging a packet of cigarettes out of a pocket as he went.

Desmond anxiously awaited his return He wanted to talk to this man who touched a musical chord in his being. He tried to speak with him as he re-entered the hall but had difficulty following what he was saying, because of the thickness of his Jamaican accent. He noticed that the bass-man grimaced as if in pain as he headed off in the direction of the bar.

"Des, why don't you talk to the old man? He seemed to know something about him," suggested Lola. The old man redirected Desmond to Blossom's uncle. "You must talk to Winston cause he know most 'bout Bassman."

According to Winston, Bassman turned up one day at a pub in Nottingham, a favourite drinking hole of some Caribbean workingmen. He sat alone, drank alone and ate alone. He wore dark glasses and a beret from which spilled tangled matted hair.

He attracted the curiosity of some of the regulars in the pub. One man went over to speak with him but the stranger turned his head and looked away. When the man stood up to leave, the stranger asked, "You know where I could find a room to rent?" The man was one of Winston's workmen and knew that Winston had a basement flat for rent but hesitated to recommend it.

"What's your name, son?" he asked.

"Bassman," replied the stranger in a deep, quiet voice.

The workman rang Winston, who agreed to see the man who called himself Bassman.

"He looked to me like he needed help and he had no problem with the two weeks rent I ask him for. He might have been down but he wasn't out, so I take him in," said Winston. "The Friday night I take him down to the club with me to let him meet some young Caribbean people who trying to live positive lives, you know what I mean?"

The youth club would become the place where Bassman went in his spare time, to play dominoes, cards and draughts, listen to music and conversation. Through contact at the club he found a job in a Jamaican record shop; he could listen to music all day and get paid for it. He bought a CD player and whenever he was at home there was music coming from his flat. His choice of music was eclectic but he seemed to favour jazz and reggae. Then one day he came back from a weekend trip lugging an old double bass case.

Winston saw him as he arrived home and shouted out, "What you got there, man?"

"Mi double bass, man," he replied and Winston saw him smile for the first time.

Desmond wanted to hear more from Winston but the band was ready to restart. The musicians took the stage but there was no Bassman; the singer now played the bass. It was the same instrument but in the hands of the second stringer it walked now instead of running, it hummed instead of singing. An amateur had replaced a virtuoso.

"He must have one of his headaches. He seems to be getting them more often," said Winston.

"Let's go find him," said Lola, standing up and looking around the room. Desmond and Winston followed her and they set out in search of Bassman. They found him in the service area. He was slumped in a chair, his upper body spread over a stainless steel table, hands outstretched and his head resting on a side on the cold surface. He seemed semi-conscious. Lola checked his wrist then his neck for a pulse, lifted an eyelid and peered into the eye for a moment.

"He will come out of it soon," said Winston.

"This man needs a doctor," said Lola.

"He don't have no doctor, miss. Lord knows how many times I tell him to go and see a doctor."

"Call an ambulance," she said, "bring me some ice and a towel."

Desmond watched Lola's calm confidence as she took charge of the situation until the ambulance arrived, his face a picture of admiration.

Desmond and Lola returned to London the following day as Lola had to be back at the hospital for work the Monday morning. Desmond had another week before returning to his job as a schoolteacher.

ॐ❦

"The doctor say he got a tumour on his brain," Winston said to Desmond on the telephone.

"Did they give any indication how serious his condition might be?" asked Desmond.

"It serious, man, it serious," replied Winston.

Desmond poured himself a scotch and downed half of it before calling Lola with the news. In a matter-of-fact tone she said, "I suspected as much and had a discussion with Mr. Killick, our head of neurosurgery. He said that if the diagnosis was confirmed, he would be willing to see him. I'll come by you after work."

"That would be great. I asked Winston to have a look in Bassman's flat to see if he can find anything that might identify him."

Winston's search turned up a railway ticket stub from King's Cross Station, a few photos and a British Army document bearing the name Reginald Oliver. Desmond thanked Winston but said, "Getting personal information out of the army on one of its ex-members may take time. Would you talk to the fellows at the club and his colleagues at the music shop?"

కావ్

Desmond opened the door to greet Lola. He paused and eyed the two suitcases next to her. "Where are you going with those?"

"Today, I said yes to a question my mother asked me when I first told her about you, so I am moving in with you."

"What was the question, may I ask?"

"Does your head approve of your heart's choice?"

Desmond's smile turned into a laugh. "Come on in," he said. They melted into a long silent embrace until Desmond whispered into her ear, "and don't ever stop surprising me."

He brought Lola up to date over dinner

"I spoke to Mr. Killick again and he really wants to help. You would not believe what he told me. He said, 'That man is an artist, just like me.'"

A fellow at the club informed Winston that Bassman was once a marine and recalled how Bassman had broken up a fight at the club one night. There was an argument and one youth pulled a knife. Bassman moved quickly to separate them and the knifeman swung at him. Bassman grabbed him by the wrist and propelled him to the ground in a flash. The knife clattered away. The youth yelped. Bassman's boot was on his neck, a firm hand gripped his wrist while a thumb pressed into the fleshy pressure point at the base of the youth's thumb. Bassman dropped the hand and dashed out of the club.

The fellow said that Bassman had lost his best buddy in Afghanistan a few years ago, but that "He couldn't talk about it, man, he just couldn't talk about it."

Winston called the next evening to say he may have found something important at the music shop. One of the employees found a stamped letter there addressed to a Mr. Grantley Lewis in North London. It was in Bassman's handwriting and had been in the shop for some time. Bassman simply hadn't posted it.

"Let me write that address down, Winston. Please put the envelope in a larger envelope and post it to me first class. I will hand deliver it. Lola's hospital was in touch with your hospital there today. We have to get Bassman to London."

Desmond found a Grantley Lewis in the telephone directory and called the number. A woman answered the telephone and at the mention of Reginald Oliver's name, she blurted out, "He is my husband's son. Is he all right?" Mrs. Lewis spoke quickly and before Desmond could answer her question she continued, "His father has been so worried about him."

Desmond spent some time on the phone with Mrs. Lewis. Her husband was not at home. He explained how he had met Reginald, what an incredible musician he was and what had happened at the wedding in Nottingham.

"Musician? What are you talking about? Reginald liked music, he spent a lot of time listening to music and he played bass guitar a little bit, but he was no outstanding musician."

"Oh, Mrs. Lewis, your stepson is an incredible bass player. He is world-class."

"That's unbelievable."

"Mrs. Lewis, Reginald wrote a letter to his father, it is in Nottingham. It should be with me tomorrow. I would like to hand deliver it and to speak with you and Mr. Lewis."

They met at the St. Maurice Hospital the following afternoon and chatted while they awaited the arrival of the patient from Nottingham. Grantley Lewis looked to be in his mid-fifties, with a full head of hair greying at the temples. Mrs Lewis was a petite Douglah who had not lost anything of her St. Lucian accent in spite of living in Britain for over 30 years. They were sombre as they exchanged greetings and the Lewises expressed their gratitude to Desmond and Lola for their interest. "You are so kind," said Mr. Lewis.

"I was blown away by your son's playing. I am a fan. I want to hear him play again."

Desmond handed the letter to Mr. Lewis, who walked a few steps toward a brighter light and proceeded to read his son's words. Mr. Lewis wiped the back of his right hand across his eyes; his left hand fell to his side holding the letter loosely and he leaned his head against the wall. Mrs Lewis went over to her husband; he stuck out his hand and gave her the letter without saying a word.

❦❧

In a small suite of the Park Hotel, a small group of journalists and well-wishers listened intently to Desmond Belgrave as he read extracts from a book.

"The fire-fight lasted about an hour and a half. When the shooting stopped, we approached the low walls and entered the compound. There were only the dead and the wounded there. The occupants had left when the Taliban arrived and the Taliban had left when the fire got too hot for them, fleeing through the ditches screened by poppy fields on one side and corn fields on the other, a journey between life and death. They had lost this skirmish but we knew that soon there would be another and another.

I saw a wounded Taliban sitting on the ground with his back against the wall. His shirt was soaked with blood in the area of his lower abdomen. He kept staring at me. Perhaps he never saw someone this black before, I thought. Tired eyes beckoned me. I approached him slowly, keeping my eyes on his hands and my finger on the trigger of my L85. In a weak yet angry tone he asked me, 'What are you doing here?'

"I am a British Marine," I told him.

His head lolled to one side and he said, "Our fight is not with you people"

Immediately, Neville Warner flashed across my mind. I heard his London accent and saw his Kalinago features. He had stopped describing himself as Carib. God, why did his parents ever leave Dominica? And now, how I wished that the roadside bomb that blew him apart had known that this fight was not with our people. Then I yelled, "Medic, medic over here."

Desmond closed the book, looked up at his audience a broad smile on his oval face. The audience applauded.

The master of ceremonies announced the main speaker and the group focused their attention on a tall figure as he stood to address them from the head table. He was flanked by two persons. On the table there was a wide tent card on which was printed in bold letters, "People's Press Publishing Company." Off to the sides were posters of a book cover with photos of a musician, a soldier and a young boy on a surfboard, the same person at different stages of his life. The book title spread across the posters was "Helmand and Back."

"Ladies and gentlemen, my name is Reginald Oliver and I want to thank you for attending this book launch. I owe my presence here today to a group of people, seated in the front row, I would like them to stand when I call their names. Professor Peter Killick: three years ago he successfully removed the tumour from my brain and with it my musical talent. Thanks and no thanks,

Prof." He paused until the ripple of gentle laughter faded, the cameras stopped flashing and Professor Killick regained his seat.

"Fortunately there are a few YouTube videos to remind me of my bass playing days. My father, Grantley Lewis, and my stepmother, Dorothy, have been incredibly supportive. Mr. Winston Morgan, who during my time in Nottingham acted-I am using Desmond Belgrave's words here and I hope I get this right, *in loco parentis*. Thank you, Winston. Dr.Yashawini Gopwani whose patient therapy helps me to approach normalcy, helps me to live again. In fact, it was Dr. Gopwani's insistence that I put on paper the things that I saw, the things that I dreamt and thought about that formed the basis for the writing of this book. And finally but by no means least, Desmond Belgrave who read so well three extracts from my book, and his wife, super nurse Lola. Nigeria's loss is truly our gain, Lola. Desmond and Lola played critical roles in getting me the treatment I needed at all levels over the last three years and of course I could not have turned my scraps of notes into a book without Desmond's assistance. Lola says that I even speak like Des now." He paused briefly then said, "There is one more person I wish to thank. Thank you, Moyna, for forgiving me." He paused again at this point, then continued. "And you can find out more about these good people when you read the book."

His speech was a bit heavy-tongued, slow and deliberate, and his cheeks puffed with each word, like a small bellows being gently squeezed. He was clean-shaven; his hair cut low exposed a long scar over his left ear. He looked his twenty-eight years, a surprise to people who knew him when he was Bassman and looked so much older.

"My book is primarily about my personal battle with post-traumatic stress disorder. But it is also about the phenomenon of how something as deadly as a brain tumour may accentuate artistic talent."

He continued for another seven minutes and then took questions from his audience.

First journalist: "Forgive us if we ask questions that you may have answered in your book. But why did you come to Britain in the first place and what on earth persuaded you to join the British Army?"

"My father and mother separated and he immigrated to Britain when I was five years old. My mother died when I was thirteen and Dad sent for me. I had some difficulty adjusting to life in Britain at that age and did not enjoy school and I suppose I rebelled. I joined up with the other rebels in my class, got into a bit of trouble and worried my father. After school he thought the army might teach me some discipline and I must say that the possibility of adventure offered by the forces excited me. Of course I never thought that I would actually go to war."

Same journalist: "Did you approve of this war?"

"You know, only those soldiers who volunteer after a war has started get to choose their wars. Normally it is the politicians who choose wars. We just fight in them. I watched my best friend die in this war. I killed people. And when I left this war, the war didn't leave me. I dreamt war; I know what terror looks like on a human face. I have seen too many bodies twisted in death. I still wake up sometimes to the roar of helicopter blades, but there are no helicopters. No, sir, I do not approve of any war and wish they did not exist, but I do understand them. The man who told me that their fight was not with 'you people' was a Yemeni. But he asked me a question that I asked myself every day I was in Afghanistan. I have dealt with this in some detail in the book."

Second journalist: "What is this war about, in your opinion?"

"I talked a lot with Desmond about this. He felt that the book would be incomplete without a discussion on the war itself. I have to admit that I did not really understand this war until I had talked it over with him and there is a section in the book which explains what I have come to believe. It is in the last chapter of the book. Let me find it for you."

"Wars are about possessions, land, oil and other resources. But wars are also about a less tangible possession, identity. And identity is a possession that can possess the possessor. Identity is what makes a people unique but also it is what separates us. The unique features of our identity are more powerful than the common features of our identities. The war in Afghanistan is about identity. It has its genesis in a group of people who feel that their identity is under threat and must be defended aggressively. It is the same insecurity that has fuelled the rise of the far- right in Europe and the United States of America."

Questions flew fast, now. More questions about identity and the war. Reginald began to visibly tire and resumed his seat. His answers were shorter and often ended with an exhortation to "read the book".

Relief came from an old journalist in the second row: "To change the subject, are you suggesting that very talented artists are somewhat touched on the brain?" This question produced some gentle laughter.

"Not at all, although a good argument could be put forward for this in certain cases."

The laughter increased.

Another journalist wanted to know: "Who is Moyna and why did you apologise to her?"

He looked away as if peering into the distance. "She was my girlfriend and a little after I returned from Afghanistan, I, um, I almost strangled her one night. That is when I ran away and ended up in Nottingham. To answer your next question, she has moved on with her life, went back home to Scotland and is married." Reginald stared briefly at the journalist then gently nodded his head and returned his gaze to the wider audience.

"Wasn't that journalist the Grenadian girl who was at Blossom's wedding?" whispered Desmond to Lola.

"You know, I think it is. She has lost weight and changed her hairstyle though."

"You remember what her hair looked like three years ago?"

"Of course, but I guess you weren't looking at her hair, were you?"

The questions and answers continued and eventually the final question came in the form of a statement. "There appears to be some confusion about where you were born. I heard you were Jamaican but this is disputed, I understand."

Reginald chuckled "It was my accent. I hung out with a group of Jamaicans at school in London and learned to speak perfect Jamaican. Apparently it became one of the features of the complex changes to my personality after I left the war and the PTSD began to set in. But I was born in Barbados, in a place called Bathsheba."

"We must go there soon. He has talked so much about that place," said Lola

᠌᠍ঌ᠍

Bathsheba, even on a good map, is but a dash on the side of this dot of an island called Barbados. It lies on its eastern or Atlantic coast between Foster Hall and Cattlewash and below Hackleton's Cliff. It is a quiet seaside village, home to a few farmers, fishermen and other folk. It also attracts a steady trickle of holiday makers attracted to its picturesque landscape and fresh ocean breezes.

He left her gazing at the ocean, crossed the narrow street and walked into Pops rum shop one hot Saturday afternoon. Pops studied him as he made his way to the bar. His clothes, bearing and that look of curious apprehension set him apart from the rest of the patrons. His skin tone was a lighter shade of tan but as yet untanned, indicating that he lived in a cooler climate and had not been in Barbados for very long. He wore a flowered sport shirt, Bermuda shorts and sandals with socks. "English, Canadian or maybe Bermudian," Pops told himself "I'll go for English" was his final wager with himself. And when the man opened his mouth and spoke, any lingering doubt about his nationality was removed.

"Good afternoon, I'll have a beer, thanks," he said quietly, answering the question before it was asked and with a smile which produced creases around his eyes. "And one for my wife, she will be along shortly, she is still ogling that ocean." He turned toward the door as a slender figure entered. She had closely cropped hair, dark eye-shadow and matching lip stick. Her eyes danced as they took in everything about the bar.

"Oh, Lord. That girl remind me of one of Boo Sonny girls from up the hill." Pops said to himself.

He popped the cap on two Banks beers and set them down in front of the strangers. The man removed the floppy hat he was wearing, exposing a shaven head, and took a seat on a barstool. The woman remained standing, still looking around the room, and then she walked off to study the posters on the wall.

"What part of England are you from?" asked Pops.

"It's that obvious, is it?" He interpreted Pops raised eyebrows, tilt of the head and half smile as a yes. "It's funny. I have lived in England all my life and there they call me a West Indian, now I come to the West Indies and everyone calls me an Englishman." He paused for a moment, reflecting on what he had just said. "My passport tells me that I am British. So that is my nationality. But my father was born in Guyana, my grandmother in Brazil and my grandfather was born right here in Barbados." He paused again momentarily. "To answer your question, I live in Surrey but I was born in a place called Hackney. Ever heard of it?"

"Well, my brother used to drive a bus to and from a place he called 'Ackney.' Would that be near Hackney?" They both broke out in laughter. Pops threw back his bald head and exposed a flash of gold teeth. The stranger sputtered as he tried not to lose the beer he had just sipped. Still chuckling, the stranger said, "I am Desmond, Desmond Belgrave and my wife is Lola."

Pops took his outstretched hand and replied, "They call me Pops round here." He paused then nodding in the direction of the slender figure across the room, asked softly, "your wife from Barbados?"

"Oh, no, she is Nigerian."

"I am an Ibibio," Lola called out from across the room.

"What brings you to Barbados, man?" Pops asked. Bathshebans were always curious about those who chose to stay there. The west and south coasts of Barbados offered, in abundance, the amenities desired by most visitors. But Bathsheba visitors tended to be nature lovers or artists or other types who generally craved a remote location or greater interaction with a local community. Often they were people with a story.

"I'd love to tell you. It's a long story. Do you have the time?"

The New Sybaris

In the year 2015, Barbados was still emerging from the recession of 2008 and concomitant fallout, job losses, business closures, and drop off in real estate values. On the east coast in the charming seaside village of Bathsheba, there had been some changes since the economic crisis. There was a new Atlantis Hotel, smartly rebuilt on the site of the old 19th-century location. Some elements of the old Atlantis had been retained; patrons still looked out over the old train tracks and what was left of the village fishing fleet to the expanse of the Atlantic Ocean. The most significant change was the old Atlantis clientele. There were now far fewer locals and a much greater presence of the west coast smart set, newly wealthy British, North American and European tourists, many of whom were annual visitors and some of whom had purchased homes in Barbados. After lunching at Atlantis they were often seen walking along the path of the old railway track into the village and back, admiring the ocean and the giant mushroom rock formations at the water's edge. Sometimes some of them found their way into Pops' rum-shop to take in a bit of local atmosphere.

The smart set drove smart cars, of course, so there was nothing unusual when one afternoon a black Mercedes SUV slowly made its way down Cleavers Hill. At the bottom of the hill the Mercedes did not follow the road along the Bathsheba coast; instead it headed straight on to an area of private property and up to the remains of the foundations of a long-demolished structure. It was an open piece of land, a place where people gathered throughout the day to enjoy the scenery, and a favourite stop for taxi drivers taking visitors on tours of the island. This spot offered panoramic views of Bathsheba and beyond. To the left one could see as far as Pico Tenerife and to the right, the Bathsheba seafront with its giant stone heads jutting out of the shallows. Four people emerged from the air-conditioned SUV into the warm breeze coming off the Atlantic. The driver faced the ocean, arms outstretched, touching the air, smelling its invigorating mixture of salt, seaweed and the remains of dead fish.

"Do you feel that?" he asked his passengers. "Lovely, isn't it?"

There was a chorus of yeas and the four walked into the wind in the direction of the edge of the property overlooking the ocean. Off to their right, about a dozen surfers bobbed in the water. Some rose and fell while others rode the waves all the way to the shore, much to the excitement of a handful of onlookers. It looked like a typical afternoon Bathsheba scene but for a low dark cloud in the distance over the water.

The group of three men and one woman breathed in the refreshing air and took in their surroundings. The driver was a man about five-foot, eight inches tall with collar-length shiny black hair brushed straight back, a long narrow nose and an impressive suntan. He displayed many of the trappings of new wealth: Gucci loafers, gold Rolex, silk shirt, Sea Island cotton slacks, and a pair of sunglasses, the cost of which ought to have made him a seer. Indeed, some Bajans would have considered themselves privileged to earn in a year the value of the outfit and accessories the driver wore that day. He led the group to the edge of the property, paused then turned, urging the others to look inland at that section of the hill to the right of the road they had just descended. The hill was dotted with houses of various descriptions, from the simplest of Bajan chattel houses at the top, some propped on loose stone foundations, to hard-wood holiday homes, to old bay houses. One house, freshly painted and well maintained, stood out from the rest.

"Can you imagine what that would look like with all Moresco-Espagnol-type villas and condos?" The driver spread out an arm in the direction of the hill as he spoke then pointed toward the ocean. "Each one with a view of that?"

"It would be striking, but is it doable, David?" mumbled Andreas Pos. He was a very tall thin man with sandy blond hair, bushy eyebrows and gentle eyes. He wore a red Polo shirt, knee-length shorts and a pair of thick rubber slippers on two very big feet. Andreas, they all called him Andy, was Swiss and mumbled in all of the five languages he spoke, a trait, which when coupled with his preference for casual attire, tended to disguise the sharp intellect that had earned him a reputation as one of the most outstanding lawyers in London, where he had lived for the last twenty years.

"Andy, my friend, success in business is the art of the doable and you have known me for a long time now. You know my track record. What I am planning to do here has been done on the west coast of Barbados, albeit with fewer landowners. But this would be a unique site. There is nothing on the west coast like it because you don't have such steep hills so near to the ocean. The slope permits a tiered development, which will give every villa a view of the ocean," replied David King.

106

He spoke with a somewhat gentrified but still clearly identifiable London East-end accent. There was a brief silence as the group tried to envision the site as David saw it.

A squat man with a receding hairline, in-between taking photographs, spoke up in a New York accent. "I think what Andy is trying to get at is how do you plan to get the people who are there now to give up this view."

David turned to Alfred Karlfeldt and said, "It's rather simple. We offer them a little above current market value for their spot of land and we build them a replacement house in another location on a similar size lot. They end up with a new and improved home plus money in the bank. It's an offer they can't refuse."

"I would take the money and run," said the lone female in the group.

"It wouldn't be the first time, Phyllis," said David.

Phyllis Gertler, née Jordan, was also the only Bajan in the group. In her late thirties, she was twenty-plus years younger than David King. She was his woman of the moment and he was her man of the moment. She had lived in Europe for several years pursuing a modelling career but never made it big. Instead she had married a Swiss banker, a friend of Andy's. She divorced well and now divided her time between homes in Zurich and Barbados and travelling. She was a striking figure; about five-foot eight inches tall, with a skin tone a darker shade of bronze. Full lips and big almond eyes endeared her to the camera but, it had been said, her backside was a little too plump for some European runways. No one ever said that directly to her but an agent once asked her, "have you ever thought of working in Brazil?" Standing in the blustery Bathsheba breeze, her extended hair blowing in the brisk gusts, she was a picture of wild elegance.

"Well, David, if you can manage the acquisitions, given your track record, Karlfeldt Financing Corporation will give you the usual support. But the acquisitions are entirely at you."

"Hugh Turner is doing the searches to identify all the owners and will make the approaches; we won't need an estate agent. He has already found a place we can move them to. Hugh is a real doer and one of the best lawyers I have ever come across, no disrespect to present company, Andy. What you do internationally, he does locally," said David.

"Hugh is a good lawyer, but I handle far more complex situations than could possibly exist in this small island, and there is no pace, no urgency, here; no disrespect," mumbled Andy. "Now, if we can get back to the matter at hand. Do you anticipate any objections to the project?"

"Not at all," David said dismissively. "We have had no problems on the west coast with this kind of development. The local community is happy to see their people make some money and, of course, the homeowners and their family are over the moon. The new home is always the clincher."

The certainty of David's response masked its glibness and did not generate question or comment.

"How did poor people on the west coast end up owning such valuable property?" asked Alfred.

"Barbados' original source of wealth was sugar and poor people were permitted to live anywhere sugar cane didn't grow, like sandy areas or rocky hillsides like this," responded Phyllis. "Then, with the arrival of tourism, some poor people were sitting on small fortunes."

"What will you call the development, David?" said Alfred.

"I have some ideas but I haven't made a decision yet."

"I have an idea," said Andy. He paused, blank faced, while the others looked at him expectantly. "New Sybaris." He waited for their reaction like a gambler who had just tossed a hard card on the table.

"New Sybaris. What is that?" said Phyllis.

"Sybaris was the name of a Greek colony on the gulf of Taranto in southern Italy. It was home to many wealthy residents and was known as a place of luxurious living, a place for pleasure seekers," replied Andy.

"Ooh, I like the sound of that," said David. "Can you send me an email with all the relevant information?"

"Sybaris? It sounds too much like syphilis to me," said Phyllis, prompting some gentle laughter until David said, "You know, people named Phyllis shouldn't make jokes about syphilis."

Andy spluttered, his face turning bright red, and Alfred turned away stifling a laugh. Phyllis looked as if she had been slapped in the face. "It's a bit late for you to be thinking that, isn't it?"

"Surely you know by now when I am joking, luv, don't you?"

"Every skin teet ain't a laugh," said Phyllis, resorting to dialect expression as she often did when angry or when bartering in a Bridgetown market. "I take it that we have finished talking about your project now."

"Hey, chaps, let's head back to Ping Wing," said David, referring to his west coast villa, christened after the local name for a type of Pandanus, a large

108

plant with wild-looking, long serrated-edged leaves found all over the island and on the borders of his own property.

The exchange between Phyllis and David seemed to dampen the mood of the group and they proceeded to the Mercedes in quiet single file.

"Does anyone know how this place ended up with a Jewish name, Bathsheba?" asked Alfred as they reached the SUV.

"Oh, there is a legend," Phyllis said. "It may even be true, that some official, way back when, saw three naked women bathing in the surf and it made him recall the biblical story of King David and Bathsheba."

"King David, David King. That's kind of creepy," said Andy. There was laughter again as the four drove off.

As the SUV slowly climbed the hill, leaving Bathsheba behind, the rain cloud arrived, darkening the landscape, and water poured from the skies.

A week later, on a sunny windless afternoon, the whir of spinning blades mingled with engine noise overpowered the gentle splashing of the Bathsheba surf. The helicopter came in low and hovered near the shoreline. A photographer was lying on the floor of the helicopter, his lens jutting out of the open door. People on the ground paid little attention to him. It was not that unusual an event. Bathsheba was one of the most photographed parts of the island.

అ఼ఌ

Three months later, Elroy DaCosta Gaskin walked into Pops' rum-shop one Friday evening. He spotted Tony Holford, the man he was looking for, sitting at the bar chatting with Pops. He approached Tony and spoke in a quiet tone and with an expression that suggested his matter was important. "Schools, I could have a word with you in private?" Tony, a university graduate, was known as Three Schools or Schools in the village.

"Sure, Rabbit," Tony replied, using Elroy's better known nickname. Rabbit had come to the man in the village whom many relied on for consultation on official matters. Tony was naturally empathetic, would write letters for people or assist with filling in forms, or often he was just a good ear. They moved to an outside table for privacy.

"What's going on, Rabbit?"

"A man and a woman come to see me yesterday. They tell me that some Englishman want to buy my house and he offering me two hundred thousand dollars and he going to build a new house for me in Foster Hall. I want to know if you think that is enough money. He say that I could talk to a lawyer but shouldn't talk to nobody else."

Tony stared out toward the ocean as if he was seeking inspiration for his response from the white caps or from the giant stone heads scattered along the shore. Rabbit was patiently studying Schools' elongated ebony face with its droopy eyelids. He sensed uncertainty or conflict or both in his friend's silence.

"Who were the people, Rabbit? Didn't they give you their names or leave a card?"

"Yes, the man give me a card," he said, fishing in his pocket. "Here, the woman name Phyllis, she real pretty, but she didn't tell me she last name. They was real nice people."

Tony studied the card briefly. It read: *Roderick Springer, Attorney-at-Law, Prudence Chambers.*

"Prudence. That is Hugh Turner's Chambers. He took over after Prudence Jackman died. Tell me something, Rabbit: Did these people talk to anyone else on the hill?"

"Well, nobody ain't tell me nothing, but when they left my house I see they went down the hill to Boysie and Thelma."

Tony did not know any Roderick Springer but he was familiar with Prudence Chambers. They specialized in commercial matters and represented some of the west and south coast developers who built luxury villas and condominiums there.

"Rabbit, these people just don't want your property. They want all the properties on the hill. They have bought up all of the west coast and the south coast and now they are coming for us, we are being encircled, surrounded. You haven't heard anything from any of the other people on the hill, have you?"

"Nothing at all, not a word."

Tony took the packet of cigarettes out of his shirt pocket and tapped one out. He placed the cigarette in his mouth but did not light it.

Tony contemplated the situation. Over the last forty years, the continual building of condominiums and villas in-between the hotels along the St. James, St. Peter and Christ Church coastlines had become lucrative but controversial in Barbados. It was lucrative for owners of beach-front properties who agreed to sell them at rates unimaginable previously; for real estate agents; for developers who could become wealthy from a single project; for construction companies, lawyers, architects, engineers and other related suppliers of goods and services to the these projects. And it was lucrative for the government, which, even though it waived import duties on the building materials, collected monies while the projects were being developed and in perpetuity from land taxes, value added taxes, national insurance contributions and income tax from all the various players in addition to whatever was generated by visitors staying in these accommodations.

It was controversial to many Barbadians who bemoaned the loss of beach access and views of the sea as one drove along the coast. It also concerned environmentalists worried about the impact of such large-scale construction in close proximity to the shoreline. Some sociologists saw the development as a continuum of the colonial experience and speculated on the social implications of more Blacks working in service capacities for Whites, as almost all purchasers in these enterprises were white.

"Rabbit, let me get back to you tomorrow on this."

"Schools, I feel I should double the price they offering, these kind o' people got nuff money. What you say?"

"How much you paid for that house?"

"I build that in 1979 for thirty thousand dollars and I pay off everything now, I ain't owe that house a penny now."

Tony nodded. "Let us talk tomorrow. I will come to you."

Tony got up and returned to the bar to pay his tab. He thought of asking Pops a question but decided against it. Pops would certainly have spoken to him if he had already heard. He headed home and checked the telephone directory for an old school friend, Peter Devonish. Peter and his wife, Monica, owned *Casa De Carlos*, a villa near the bottom of the hill, and were most likely to know what was going on. He reached Peter, who said that he had not heard anything, but "Hugh Turner invited Monica to lunch on Monday and obviously that is what he wants to talk to her about." Monica was not in at that moment but he would tell her when she got in.

Peter could sense the worry in Tony's voice. He thought of the Tony that he knew, the Tony who captained the school's cricket team and opened the batting to some of the island's most fearsome fast bowlers in the days when Barbados had fearsome fast bowlers. He was calm, confident and brave in those days, but he sounded rattled now.

"Let's stay in touch with each other," said Peter.

111

"Yes," said Tony. He hung up the phone, poured himself a rum and water, went on to the veranda of his home and sat in a rocking chair. He lit a cigarette. Tony wished that he was not on his own, that Grace had not left him and returned to Jamaica, taking Joshua with her. He remembered her last words to him: "I cannot let a son watch his father drink himself to death." He got up from his chair, took two steps to the veranda's balustrade, raised the glass, slowly turned his wrist and poured the rest of his drink over the silver-dollar bush below.

Tony had been raised in a protective household, but away at university and no longer under the strict supervision of his parents he discovered new pleasures in life which overwhelmed any defences his upbringing had provided and which would in time possess him.

After his return to Barbados he rented a house in Bathsheba. His parents were disappointed that he chose to live so far away from the Bridgetown suburb where they lived. When the owner of the house died, Tony purchased it from his daughter who lived overseas. It was one of the houses along the ridge opposite Andromeda Gardens. It was a small, attractively painted Greenheart house with a narrow veranda that ran the length of its front. It had a commanding view of the Atlantic and the Bathsheba coast.

Tony looked out over Bathsheba with its scattering of twinkling lights and imagined it with an array of lights, swimming pools and an entirely different population. If they took the hill on the other side of the village, it would only be a matter of time before they came for his hill.

And his adopted village, this corner of Barbados that he fell in love with all those years ago, would never be the same again. The community he had become a part of, these people who often sought his counsel, this ocean that he loved to watch and swim in early on mornings, all this would change for him. It was change he most definitely did not want to see. "They must be stopped," he told himself. "But how?"

He went back inside and picked up the telephone.

తోక

Sheri Gooding parked her car outside Tony's house. The trip from her St. Philip home had taken her about twenty-five minutes. Tony got up from his rocking chair, stubbed out his cigarette and embraced her as she arrived on the patio. Sheri was about five-foot, five inches tall with a round face, round forehead and healthy-looking waist-length dreadlocks tied behind her neck. She moved easily in spite of her few extra pounds. She wore an old pair of jeans and a tee-shirt. Sheri was a journalist with the *Daily Standard*, the island's most read newspaper.

"What's up, Tony. You sounded stressed on the phone. What's this story you want to talk to me about?"

Tony recounted his conversations with Rabbit and Peter.

"Tony, Errol Barrow said that one day we would wake up and find that this country was no longer ours. We will soon have to change the words to the National Anthem to *These fields and hills beyond recall are* **no longer** *our very own.* That Hugh Turner, I know things about him that I could never print. I am a friend of a friend of his last ex-wife. He is a perverted, misogynistic brute. Get me a drink and let us talk strategy."

"Forgive my manners, girl," Tony said. The telephone started to ring as he was making his way back. He handed Sheri her drink, turned and hurried to answer the phone.

"You need a cordless phone," Sheri shouted after him.

It was Monica Devonish. She spoke as soon as Tony picked up. "My grandfather would turn in his grave, Tony. And I will tell that reprobate Hugh Turner so when I see him Monday. He used to clerk for my grandfather before he joined Prudence Chambers, you know. My grandfather thought highly of him, but he has changed beyond recognition, seduced by money and the lifestyle of the rich and famous. And I don't buy any lawyer-talk about he is only representing his client. We don't exist in a vacuum. We are part of a community, a small one at that, and we must consider the interests of the community as a whole. That kind of thinking is beyond him, of course. You ever wondered why whenever they arrest prostitutes in Bridgetown somebody from his chambers turns up at court? Big business and small prostitutes are a part of his clientele. Big business pays him big bucks and it is alleged, Tony, it is alleged that his chambers' work for the hookers is pro bono. Pro whose bono, I wonder?"

Tony picked up a pencil and notepad from next to the telephone and started writing.

Sheri wandered into the house, empty glass in hand. There were books everywhere, on a row of shelves around the room at the height of the top of the doors, on upright book shelves and surrounding the chess set with an unfinished game on a huge coffee table. Sheri paused in front of some photos on the wall. There was a young Tony in full cricket gear heading out to open the batting with his partner. There was a dreadlocked Tony with wife and son.

"But Paul would be the perfect person to lead the charge on this," Tony said in an argumentative tone.

Sheri scanned the bookshelf, occasionally picking out a book and leafing through it.

"Look, you don't have to like the man to recognize his worth on something like this," argued Tony.

Sheri picked up Richard Allsopp's *Dictionary of Caribbean English Usage* and searched for the word "kyaki" but it was not there.

"I will see you Monday evening," Tony said after about twenty minutes. He hung up the phone, continued writing on his notepad then turned toward Sheri, brow furrowed.

"Why did you cut off your locks, Tony?"

"I decided I was not a Rastafarian, as simple as that."

"So it wasn't because they used to call you Ras Holie?" asked Sheri, a hand reaching behind her head to caress her dreadlocks.

Tony steupsed. "Listen, I didn't invite you here to talk about me."

"And what's the real reason they call you *Schools* or *Three Schools*?"

Tony laughed. "I used to beat everybody at draughts down at Pops. Then, one evening, an old man from St. John came in. I couldn't win a single game against him. At the end he stood up, stretched and said, 'I only went to one school but I beat a three schools man today.' Now, back to our business. I had an interesting conversation with Monica Devonish. We have some disagreement but she is definitely on our side. You know, I wasn't sure what position she would take when I spoke to Peter. I just thought that since they were homeowners that they would know what is going on. But boy she was hot and does not have much time for Hugh Turner; she is seeing him on Monday and coming to see me later that evening. This is not a straightforward matter. In spite of promises by politicians to reserve the east coast for development by locals only, nothing has ever gone through parliament. So, as it is, there is no restriction on the sale of private property, you cannot tell any citizen who to sell or who not to sell his or her property to."

"Monica is a good bougie, you know," said Sheri.

"What's a bougie?

"It's youth slang for bourgeoisie. I learned that from my son. Monica doesn't want you to involve Paul Kyaki in this, huh?"

"Not directly. But she will leak the story to him. I am cool with that. Kyaki will take this and run with it."

Sheri had reflected on the man known as Paul Kyaki while Tony was on the phone. Paul had been sent to the USA to study medicine but disappointed his parents by switching to journalism. He was known as Paul Edwards then. Kyaki was a nickname given to him sometime after his return to Barbados. In America he had been involved in student politics and the civil rights movement. The week after Martin Luther King, Jr. was assassinated he abandoned his studies and left the country. After he returned to Barbados he worked as a journalist for a while. He gave that up after his father died and left him a couple of properties in Bridgetown which Paul's grandfather had acquired with Panama money. The rents plus some freelance work and his wife's income were enough for them to live on and gave him time to pursue his political activism. He was a constant letter writer to the press. He allied himself with various pressure groups but never seemed to find a space he wanted to occupy permanently. Paul's experiences in the USA had produced strong anti-American views and an embrace of America's foes. Any enemy of America became his friend, including autocratic and totalitarian leaders under whose regimes he could not have survived given his outspoken nature.

Sheri understood Monica's thinking that Paul's direct support could be counterproductive but agreed that he would be the perfect public voice of the opposition to the Bathsheba project.

"Let us leak it to him, instead," Monica had told Tony. In any case, the only politician they wanted to talk to was Tony's former boss when he was in the ministry of finance, the Prime Minister.

"I agree with a lot of Paul's criticisms of Barbados," Sheri said. "My problem with him is the kind of solutions he thinks we need here. I know that I could no longer do my job as a journalist if he were ever to achieve political power. I might even end up in jail."

"That's nonsense, Sheri."

"Oh, yeah? We should ignore the tyranny that he has supported over the years? When your political heroes include Gaddafi, Mugabe and the like, what conclusions should we draw? That once you have battled colonialism, you get a pass for life, a pass to inflict terror on your own people, the people you came to save? I don't know how he reconciles his advocacy of freedoms here with his support for repression elsewhere. But I know it ought to be a reason never to put political power in his hands." Sheri extended both hands and, palms upwards, bounced them up and down, then continued. "They say that the trouble with ideologues is they buy into a package of ideas and after that, they no longer think outside of the box those ideas came in. They permit a bunch of dead people to do their thinking for them. Paul is so predictable that two of our young reporters play a game, a contest to see who can more closely write his response to their question before they call him. They are often so close that their version could be used."

"Look, look, we have been down this road before. Let us focus on the immediate threat."

They returned to talking about Bathsheba.

After Tony saw Sheri off, he went to bed. As he laid thinking about the evening's events, his hand dangled over the side. He thrust his hand under the bed, grabbed the rum bottle there by its neck and brought it up to his face. He stared at the label then sighed and put the bottle back under the bed.

Tony walked down to the beach early the next morning, passing other early-rising neighbours who were already getting on with chores. One neighbour was feeding his black-belly sheep, another was hanging out clothes and a couple of fishermen were heading down to Tent Bay, where their boats were moored. This morning, Tony did not stop to chat with any of them. He shouted out quick greetings and went on his way. At the beach he did not spend much time with the usual group. He did some stretching, jogged up and down a few times then did a brisk swim and took his leave. He headed over to *Casa De Carlos*, where he found Rabbit raking the yard.

"Hi, Rabbit. I promised to get back to you with an answer to your question. Listen, I want you to do something for me. Call that lawyer, Springer, and ask him to tell you the name of the person who wishes to buy your house. If he refuses, tell him that you don't want to do business with some person who wants to hide their identity and that he should get back in touch with you when he is ready to do so. If he tells you who the client is, I would like you to share that information with me. You definitely need legal advice and the obvious person for you to talk to would be Monica Devonish.'

"You right for true. I going talk to Miss Monica."

"You know, it could be one of your neighbours trying to buy you out and this Foster Hall thing could be a smoke screen. Try to find out from your neighbours what they have been told as well. You really don't know what is going on until you know who you are dealing with, my friend."

"You right, Schools. I going do what you tell me. You know it could be Englishman, old Miss Eversley son, who just come back from England. I hear he looking for some place to build in the area."

"We don't know that, Rabbit, but we must try to find out. Talk to you later, buddy."

As Tony left Rabbit he thought of Monica. He had executed the first tactic of their strategy. She had told him that in order to get Rabbit to cooperate, "You have to sow doubt in his mind. Get him to make Turner's associate to reveal the client's name and get him to call me. Tell him to talk to his neighbours; Hugh wants to keep this secret as long as possible. You already have the press lined up, that is a good move, Tony, but hold her back until you have more irrefutable facts."

Between Saturday afternoon and Sunday morning, Rabbit spoke to all the residents of the hill and Tony initiated his second tactic. He spoke to some known opponents of the expansion of condominiums built by and developed for foreigners. He and Monica had agreed on some names. Among them were an environmentalist, a historian and a sociologist.

Tony was still working the phone in the middle of the day when Rabbit turned up at his house. He told Tony that all his neighbours had been approached and wanted to sell, though no one disclosed how much they were offered. They agreed that they wanted to know how genuine the offer was and who was behind it. Rabbit said that he would call the lawyer and report back to them.

On Sunday night Tony received a call from Paul Kyaki. They had been to the same high school but Paul was in his final year when Tony was in his first. But apart from their age difference, they would not have been friends at school as Paul's connections with people from a lower socio-economic background did not start until he became radicalized in America. The Sixties radical, had been a member of every political party in Barbados but was now an independent. In the only election he contested as an independent, he gained 17 votes. "But he is a man from a big family. You mean he couldn't even get he own family to vote for he?" a supporter of one of his political opponents commented on radio in a post-election review.

"Thanks for the call, Paul, but I still have some contacts in my old ministry. I plan to talk to the Prime Minister," said Tony.

Paul laughed. "Tony, you can't be so naïve as to believe that the government doesn't already know about this. The selling off of land to foreigners has been part of the economic strategy of both political parties for years. And when they put up the land tax in the whole of Bathsheba the rest of you will have to sell, too." He then launched into a tirade against the Prime Minister, the government and the Opposition.

Tony called Monica about the conversation with Paul. Her only concern was that Paul would go public before they were ready to do so and give Hugh Turner and his client more time to mount their defence and to dismiss Paul as a rabble-rouser who did not want poor black people to get money; a defence which they feared would dog their own efforts.

On Monday morning, Paul was walking the road in Bathsheba, knocking on doors and talking to residents. In his dashiki and afro, he could have been attending a back-in-time seventies affair. He did not get the response he was expecting. First of all there was only one resident at home on the hill and that was because she had a young baby.

"I ain't know nothing 'bout what you asking me," she said to Paul. She looked at him then looked away. Her face said more to him than her words. Paul recognized a barrier of suspicion that he could not penetrate. In the rest of the village, people genuinely did not know what he was talking about and a couple of them were clearly hostile to him, with one character in Pops' bar wanting to know, "Wait, if somebody want to buy my house and I want to sell it, what that got to do with you?"

"You could lease them your land instead of selling and in this way you never give up ownership and it remains for your grandchildren and great-grandchildren," Paul tried to explain.

"But that is my business, not yours," was the abrupt reply.

Paul decided to change tact and arranged a press conference for the following morning at 10 o'clock.

෧෧

Monica arrived at Brown Sugar restaurant on time but ahead of Hugh, who hurried in to the restaurant about 20 minutes later full of apologies. He was a tall, barrel-chested man with spindly legs which made him look top-heavy and a high forehead which seemed to stretch to the middle of the top of his head. He was fair-skinned with tight curly hair with a naturally reddish tinge. His moustache ran down into his goatee to encircle his mouth. He wore half glasses, a black blazer with a blue shirt and a white-and-blue patterned tie. Monica extended her right hand to shake his. Hugh took her hand, brought it to his lips and kissed it.

"How are you, Hugh?"

"As good as ever. How are you, my dear?"

"I am famished. Can we go straight to the buffet?"

Monica wasn't really that hungry but she had lost time waiting on Hugh and wanted to get through the lunch as quickly as possible and get back to the office.

"Yes, of course, let's go."

They made their way to the buffet. Hugh, his head bobbing to the re-corded music, seemed in a particularly good mood or maybe just trying to give the impression of being cool and relaxed. They both passed on the pumpkin soup and Hugh filled his plate with samples of everything on offer, topping it off with slices of roast pork. Monica settled for an abundance of salads, vegetables, a little sweet potato and some roast black belly lamb. They made their way back to the garden table, exchanging greetings with familiar faces as they went.

As soon as they sat down Monica asked, "So Hugh, what's up? You didn't get me here just to feed me, did you?"

Hugh looked at her askance and chuckled. "Straight to the point, just like old Reds. He taught you well."

Monica did not like him calling her long-deceased grandfather by his nickname. She felt Hugh had lost the right to such familiarity.

He continued, "I have a client who wants to buy *Casa De Carlos* and has asked me to handle the negotiations on his behalf."

"Wow. What ever made you think that my house was for sale?"

"Monica, everything is for sale for the right price. You know that."

"You can tell your client I am not interested. *Casa De Carlos* was a gift from my dear grandfather, and I have a strong emotional attachment to it."

"That is a pretty good negotiating tactic but you haven't yet heard what I am authorized to offer you for it."

"I said I wasn't interested in selling."

"Not even for two million US dollars?"

Monica looked directly into Hugh's eyes and spoke with a bitter tongue. "Hugh Turner, not even if you throw in the house in Foster Hall. Did you forget that, or were you planning to keep that spot for yourself?"

Hugh turned away from Monica's unblinking eyes. His cell phone rang. He seemed relieved as he answered. "Hello … .Oh hello, Mr. Prime Minister.…Yes, that is correct…I don't think I could make this evening and … I am in court tomorrow morning but I should be able to see you in the afternoon. Would that be all right? ….Let us say two o'clock…that is fine.…Goodbye, sir."

Monica stopped smiling as Hugh turned towards her with a perplexed look on his face.

"A call from the PM. Are you going into politics?"

Hugh ignored the question. Vacant eyes suggested his thoughts were elsewhere. He asked, "What is this about Foster Hall?"

"Attorney-client privilege, Hugh, attorney-client privilege. But you know exactly what I am talking about. Who is this client of yours who wants to buy my house, anyway?" Monica had intended to ask that question before but her dislike of Hugh had disturbed her usual calmness and control. In fact, it had changed her entire game plan. She thought that he was unlikely to say who his client was now. But he had to tell Rabbit.

Hugh was eating hurriedly and seemed not to be listening then he stopped with his fork halfway to his mouth, looked directly at Monica and said, "My client is a Lichtenstein company." He soon cleared his plate and asked to be excused as he had to return to his office.

Once in his car he called David King at his Ping Wing office. "I need to see you right away. I have to meet the Prime Minister tomorrow to discuss Bathsheba."

"Is that good or bad, Hugh?"

"Probably bad. I did warn you about the probability of negative reaction and outright opposition."

"Yes, you did, and I have planned for it. I will fill you in when you get here."

"I'll be there in about twenty minutes."

Hugh next called his secretary and asked her to clear his appointments for the rest of the day. His secretary told him that Roderick Springer wanted to speak with him.

"Put him on, Judy….Yes, Roddy, what is it?"

Roddy said that he had received a call from Elroy Gaskin.

"Who the hell is Elroy Gaskin?" interrupted Hugh.

Roddy explained that Elroy was one of the residents on the hill in Bathsheba. He wanted to know the identity of the purchaser. "I told him it was a company but he said that I had told him it was an Englishman and he needed to know who the person was before he agreed to the sale. I said that I would get back to him."

"Thanks for letting me know, Roddy. I will get back to you."

Hugh drove his BMW through the open gates, parked it under the porte-cochere and entered the villa. Ping Wing was a grand new house. David King had bought the old property in the early Eighties when he first visited Barbados and ten years later demolished it to build his tropical dream home. The new villa was designed by Rafael Ben-Younis, a Spanish architect of Tunisian descent, and was a beautiful example of Spanish-Moorish architecture. Ben-Younis had designed projects for David for many years, beginning with condos in Majorca then other parts of Spain, then North Africa and the UK, and now Barbados. An exception was a recently completed block of condos in St. Peter, where the other partners on that venture had succeeded in persuading David that Ben-Younis' concept lacked grandeur. An alternative architect produced a design with an imposing façade. Once built, it looked out of place and earned the local nickname of *King's Kong*. A combination of its obzocky frontage, the US ten million-dollar price tag of the apartments and the recession resulted in no sales for the units in spite of beautiful interiors and its prime beachfront position.

As he entered the living room he was met by Donna Quimby, David's secretary.

"Good afternoon, Mr. Turner. Mr. King is in his office."

"Thank you, Donna. You are still looking as good as ever," Hugh said, casting a leery eye over her figure.

He made his way to the right wing of the house, knocked at the door of David's pool-side office and entered. He was greeted by David, smiling. David was a man who always seemed to be in good spirits. Hugh often wondered at the source of such permanent confidence.

"Hugh, my old friend," said David, extending his hand and giving Hugh a brief but vigorous shake.

"Sorry about the short notice, Dave," replied Hugh.

"Oh, it's no problem at all. The timing is perfect. Because of the time difference, all my European communication is completed during the morning so I am very flexible any time after noon. So what's this about the Prime Minister, then? Does he want to buy one of our villas?" David said with a chuckle.

"Actually, he hasn't told me what he wants but the fact that he wishes to discuss the matter indicates to me that he has a problem with it," said Hugh.

David pushed back in his chair, ran his fingers through his hair. "I think you are right, and so was Andy."

Three months earlier, when they returned to Ping Wing after showing Andy Pos and Alfred Karlfeldt the site, Andy predicted that the project would be controversial.

"Well, you know Andy, he likes to take what he calls a wholistic approach to everything and his assessment is that there is growing discomfort among sections of the local population over the expansion of condos in Barbados and that the siting of this kind of development on the east coast would create an emotional response."

"So, what is your take on it?" Hugh asked.

"Well, I wasn't sure he was right but I have a lot of respect for Andy's opinions. I have been preparing for a backlash."

Hugh paused, thinking to himself that this man certainly didn't get to where he was by not anticipating problems.

"What is your plan?" asked Hugh.

"It depends on where the opposition is coming from. Remember, whoever opposes us will have the big problem of convincing the people on the hill that they would be better off turning down our offer; that they should give up a basic right that everyone else in this country has, to sell something that belongs to them." He paused briefly then continued: "So, the only opposition we have to worry about is from those owners and, from what you have told me, they are all interested in selling. And you mustn't forget that development has been stagnant in this island since the recession of 2008."

"You are basically right but when the Prime Minister gets involved...."

David held up his hand. "First of all, the Prime Minister is bound to uphold the laws of the land and what we are planning to do is perfectly legal. Secondly he is a politician and knows what it takes to be elected."

Hugh wondered if there might be a hint of ambiguity in the last statement but did not wish to explore the matter. Instead he said, "He not only upholds the law, David, he can also make the law."

"You are right, but he would be a foolish man to create a law to disenfranchise a particular group of his own citizens," said David, with a nod of his head.

This was a powerful argument but Hugh couldn't help wondering who had gotten to the Prime Minister so fast and how powerful they might be. His discussion with David went on for another forty-five minutes and ended with David explaining that the conceptual designs would soon be with him and he understood that they were spectacular. He asked Hugh to proceed as fast as possible with concluding the purchase of the Foster Hall site.

"Aren't you being a bit premature?"

"Foster Hall Heights will happen with or without the Bathsheba development; I could just put in roads and services and sell the lots on the local real estate market if necessary. So please go full steam ahead. The Bathsheba deal is conditional and I will set out the conditions for you. By the way, the concept drawings are just computer graphics; they are not expensive but they are powerful persuaders. Rafael has done so much work for me over the years that I may never even see a bill for them. I am told that he has outdone himself this time; you must come and see them."

David was all smiles as he said goodbye to Hugh. "Good luck with the Prime Minister. You should try to see when he is free to join us for dinner here one evening."

❧ ❧

From her office at the *Standard* newspaper, Sheri Gooding, or I-Sher as she was called at work ever since she started wearing dreadlocks, got on the phone to Tony Holford. "My editor just called me to her office to tell me that Paul Kyaki is holding a press conference tomorrow morning to discuss the developments in Bathsheba. She says that we need an article for tomorrow's paper. Do you have any more information for me?"

Sheri wanted more details, the name of the developers, exactly what they were planning to do with the site, what sort of money they were looking to invest and what kind of profits they stood to make. Tony told her she should put Hugh Turner on the spot, not him.

He then said, "I spoke to the PM and he placed a call to Hugh in my presence. They are meeting tomorrow afternoon but you shouldn't publish that. The PM is very sympathetic to our position but has some legal concerns. I believe that he also has political concerns."

ॐ

Tony greeted Peter and Monica on the veranda.

"The *Standard* is going with whatever they have of the story tomorrow, Sheri tells me. I expect you have heard of Kyaki's press conference."

Monica told Tony about her meeting with Hugh and how she lost her cool.

"I didn't think you had any cool left to lose," said Peter, chuckling.

"My supply of cool is inexhaustible, thank you, husband."

Tony said that his brief meeting with the PM left him with the impression that something would be done.

"Don't you know that politicians are masters at giving impressions," said Peter. "That is why comedians and impersonators love them so much."

They knew that the owners on the hill would need some incentive to refuse the offer to buy them out. But they could think of none. Eventually, Tony said with a smile that he had an idea.

"Let us take this to a higher power. Let us talk to Reverend Farley, see where he stands, or let us find the nearest preacher who is on our side."

"Did you say a higher power? Listen, man, I had no idea you could be this manipulative."

"Oh, I am not manipulative. I am just resourceful. Mankind has always made use of God ever since He created Him."

They all laughed and Monica said, "I think it is a brilliant idea, Tony. I don't really care for some of the Reverend's views but I'll volunteer to speak with him. He knew my grandfather well."

ॐ

On Tuesday morning the *Standard* ran the following headline:

English Developer Has Sights Set on Bathsheba

The article by Sheri Gooding included a quote from an emailed statement from Hugh Turner of Prudence Chambers in response to questions from the reporter.

"We confirm that we are representing a client who is prepared to invest millions of dollars in a small tasteful green development in the Bathsheba area. The development would be of substantial benefit to individual members of the community, the wider community as a whole and to Barbados. It is premature at this time to disclose any further details."

Paul Kyaki's press conference amounted to a harangue of government for not having enacted legislation to prevent this kind of development. "There is simply no land-use policy in this island."

The *Standard*'s front page story took the surprise element away from Paul but later in the day he managed to make it as a guest on one of the lunchtime call-in programmes and things were hot.

Call-in programmes in Barbados were dominated by a small group of people with time on their hands, a desire to be heard on any issue and a speed dial. The great majority of callers were opposed to the planned development and tried to outdo each other with claims of its consequences and about the motives of the developers.

"These people want to buy and sell us."

"They going soon got the whole island surround and we coop up in the middle in pens."

"You can't blame the poor people for wanting to get ahead but they got to look at the big picture. They are giving away our birthright."

"They going take over the whole o' Bathsheba and we won't even be able to drive down there."

"Look, the government could've stopped this long time ago and none of them did. Not the Bees, nor the Dees. You got to ask why."

Paul was delighted with the responses.

"The people are with us, the politicians will have to follow."

തെ≪

Tony Holford listened intermittently to the call-in programme at his office in Foreign Affairs, where he had been switched from Finance. It was a lateral move for him; he was well liked both by colleagues and seniors but his alcoholism had hindered his career advancement.

He felt encouraged by the overwhelming show of support but he knew that persuading people in the Bathsheba community would be another matter completely. Many of these people were close to the potential beneficiaries of the project and not only did they wish to see their friends do well but hoped that they, too, might benefit in some way from any resulting prosperity. He hoped that things would work out with the reverend.

The island was abuzz with the story. Sheri followed up her first story with an article with comments from prominent real estate agents in Barbados. All denied any knowledge of the project and surprised Sheri by siding with the 'No' camp. They did not know who the developer was, but one agent said that he had a pretty good idea who it might be.

"There is one developer I know of who likes small, very upscale developments for which he did not need a real estate agent; but I wouldn't like to call any name right now."

Some agents were willing to comment on condition that they not be identified.

Hugh Turner's meeting with the Prime Minister was short and cordial but the seriousness was clear. Hugh declined to identify his client; he said that his client would come forward at a date of his choosing. The PM wanted a clear message sent to the client. "I have received countless messages from a wide cross section of people opposed to this project." He wanted Hugh to tell his client that his actions were provocative, would be unpopular with Barbadians and could be bad for the government. He wanted a halt brought to the purchase without disclosure that the government had requested such action. He thought this was the simplest of solutions.

"I'll see what I can do, Mr. Prime Minister."

"One more thing," said the Prime Minister. "Remind him who it is that gives final planning approval for projects of this sort."

"I will, Mr. Prime Minister. But I will tell you one thing about my client. He enjoys a battle, he is not averse to litigation and he can afford it."

"That was three things, Hugh. But you can tell him one thing from me." An index finger tapped loudly on his desk. "This is my island."

෴

Everywhere people were talking about it and nowhere more so than Bathsheba. Pops' rum-shop was busy every evening with locals and every lunchtime with tourists, many of whom, responding to the newspaper articles and letters to the editor, took tours to Bathsheba.

The newspapers' letters section reflected the variety of views of callers to the radio stations but evidently people took greater care with the written than with the spoken word and arguments were better presented. One writer pointed out that Barbados was not the first and only country to face this situation; other countries had restrictions on foreigners buying property. Some countries restricted foreign ownership of property to certain zones; others stipulated that they could only buy property from another foreigner. The intention was to shield and protect the local housing market from hyper inflation caused by runaway demand for property by foreigners with very large budgets.

අංකි

Bathsheba was enjoying all the free publicity. Sam Coochie was doing a roaring trade on the beach with his paintings; he couldn't produce them fast enough. The biggest demand was for portraits of tourists with a giant Bathsheba rock and the wild Atlantic in the background. He particularly enjoyed painting the women as it gave him an opportunity to chat them up while they sat for him. He was so busy, he went advertising in Pops' rum-shop for an assistant.

"Anybody in here can draw portraits?" Sam called out. A bright-eyed young man, with corn-rowed hair and round rimless glasses, said that he could. Sam yelled out, "Good, I looking for somebody to draw the men," and joined in the laughter in and around the bar.

It was high season in the middle of low season. Two enterprising students from the community college appeared out of nowhere and were conducting walking historical tours of Bathsheba for only $10.00 a head. There were more vendors everywhere, on the beach, by the old railway café and on the hill by the community centre. The botanical gardens at Andromeda were straining with visitors. The bars were busy all day. The surfers were there to surf but also to lime and talk long into the night. And as the sun disappeared behind the hills, the aroma of marijuana wafted through the air at the western end of the village, around *Reefer's* shop.

∽✑∾

Reverend Farley wrote the title of the next Sunday's sermon on the notice board, *When the Serpent Calls,* in bold lettering. He had a packed congregation, including Peter and Monica.

"Today I speak to you about Adam and Eve. Adam and Eve were the ungrateful recipients of God's natural bounty. They had everything that nature could offer, but it wasn't enough for them. No, some people can never have enough," he said with a wave of his right hand, "so they give in to the temptations of the serpent, the viper. Adam and Eve were ignorant when it came to serpents. They did not know that the serpent could shed his skin, they did not know that when he sheds his skin and he comes back to you in a brand new and shiny coat he is still the same old snake that you were dealing with before and his intentions are the same as before. No, they did not know the ophidian like I know the ophidian. They were ignorant of his ways, and ignorance is truly a curse. In Hosea, Chapter 4, Verse 6, the Bible says, 'My people are destroyed from the lack of knowledge' and ignorance is simply that, the lack of knowledge, and it has dangerous, dangerous consequences. But while ignorance is a curse, the lack of common sense is even worse."

Reverend Farley was a big round man, evidence of too many good meals and perhaps, some said, too many glasses of communion wine. He spoke slowly, elongating words for emphasis, his voice rising and falling as he slowly rocked back and forth, movement and cadence seemingly synchronized. Sometimes he scanned the faces of his congregation, then he looked up to the heavens then out across the ocean, then he came back to them and saw that they were listening.

"In the Garden of Eden there were all kinds of good fruits. There were pineapples, there were mammy apples, there were sugar apples, there were star apples, there were golden apple trees filled with delicious fruit, yet Eve heeded the call of the rattlesnake. She heard the rattle and thought it was speaking to her. Adam, instead of providing leadership, followed her and they ate the apple of the manchineel tree, and you know what happens to those who eat the apple of the manchineel tree… their intestines become twisted as the body tries to reject the bitter poison, the venom. But it is too late, and they are condemned thereafter to a wretched and painful existence and even death."

He finally turned to the title of his sermon.

"This morning I ask you: Do you know what to do when the serpent calls? Do you? Do you give away your life for the lack of knowledge, or do you do as the Lord Jesus Christ did? There is no better example to follow, my friends. When the serpent calls, you say to the serpent, get thee hence, Satan, get thee henssse!"

He spat and hissed the final word with a vigorous shaking of his head. Many serious faces left the church that morning. There wasn't the usual chatter; instead people spoke to each other quietly and earnestly.

Peter and Monica offered their congratulations to a beaming Reverend Farley. Immediately after, they drove to Tony's to tell him about the reverend's sermon. "It deserved an Oscar. Not once did he mention the hill or the people who lived there but it was powerfully clear," said Peter.

"You know, Eve has been unfairly condemned throughout history; anyone hearing a serpent speak would surely be tempted to believe every word it said," commented Tony, a wide grin on his face.

In the next few days there were signs of a shift in public opinion within the village, though not from anyone on the hill, only one of whom had been in Reverend Farley's church Sunday morning.

Tony increased the frequency of his visits to Pops at this time. He explained to patrons that this new community would be separate from the rest of the village and that the people on the hill were unwittingly breaking up the community and would facilitate the creation of a kind of apartheid in Bathsheba. "The community will never be the same again," he warned them.

The focus of the argument had shifted from the benefits to the current residents on the hill to the relationship, or lack of, with any future residents. People in the village started asking, "Who would these people be? Exactly where would they come from? How would they treat us?"

"What do you think will happen to your land taxes?" Tony asked. This always touched a nerve with the villagers.

The politicians had been quiet except for Paul Kyaki, who announced that he had arranged a town hall meeting for the following Friday night at the community centre and was demanding to hear from the Prime Minister, who had not made any public statement on the matter.

There was a huge turnout. People came from all eleven parishes of Barbados. Before the meeting started there was argument. The size of the crowd meant that everyone could not be accommodated within the centre and some

Bathsheba people objected to being outside when people from elsewhere were inside and seated.

"Bathsheba people first, the rest of St. Joseph people next and after that any number can play," said one boisterous voice.

Paul was uncomfortable with this arrangement simply because opposition to the development was stronger outside of the village. But the villagers were insistent and the meeting threatened to descend into chaos before it even started. At the suggestion of Sheri Gooding, Paul accepted the villagers' position. "If you do not agree to the villagers' demand, you will not have a meeting tonight. Those wishing to speak can enter, have their say and then go back outside," she told him.

The outsiders were asked to go outside. Those inside, apart from the head table and media, were Bathsheba residents with a few from neighbouring villages.

The meeting started nearly an hour late. Paul spoke first. He reminded his audience that the spot on which they now stood was once home to a group of the original Amerindian inhabitants of Ichirouganaim long before this place was known as Barbados. "And they were chased off by invaders." Those who had read the letters to the press would have recognized the repetition of points made in some of them. He finished by saying, "Those who do not remember their history are bound to repeat its mistakes."

Paul was followed by a succession of speakers chosen by him. They produced a variety of arguments against the development while taking care not to say anything offensive about the residents on the hill. But one speaker called the developer, who was still un-named, a plethora of derogatory names. He was a slave master, vicious, criminal, white, bastard, white-bastard, maternal copulator (or something like that), a snake in the grass who felt he could buy and sell people.

"Why does this man not say who he is? That alone should make you suspicious of him. He must be a man of secrets and you have every right to be afraid of secretive men," said the final speaker and lone female from the head table.

As soon as the meeting was opened to the floor, some outsiders pressed to be heard. After three of them spoke in succession, the insiders rose up in complaint that they were not being permitted to respond. To everyone's surprise the normally quiet and shy Rabbit insisted on being heard and was given the floor.

130

Rabbit walked up to the head table, did a hundred-and-eighty-degree turn and with his back to it addressed the audience. "I am one of the people who live on the hill. I hope that the people here from the hill understand what is going on. These people behind me think they know what best for we, yet they don't want we to get some money, like them.

I want you to look at these people." He flung his arm backward toward the persons seated at the head table and raised his voice. "Not one o' them ain't come from 'bout here. Any of these people ever do anything for you?"

There was a loud chorus of "NO."

Rabbit said, "All right, then," and returned to his seat to applause and stamping of feet.

After Rabbit spoke, the outsiders resumed their arguments against the project, but none of the insiders seemed to be listening. Some laughed and talked among themselves during the speeches, others showed the complete range of disinterest on blank faces.

After the meeting ended, two young men were outside handing out leaflets. They were glossy, full-colour flyers depicting beautifully designed homes, some with cars in the driveways. The computer-generated images were an artist's impression of an aerial view of a new housing estate, Foster Hall Heights. People stopped in their tracks.

"Lookah. Cheese-on-bread, people like they getting cars!?" cried one Bathsheba resident. It was a cry of incredulity. He could have been asking a question or making a statement. One wasn't sure.

"Lemme see that," said a young woman. "Oh rass-hole. Listen, wunnuh sell wunnuh houses, hear. Don't mind de foolish people out here. Some o' dem ain't got nuttin and they ain't want you to get nuttin."

The two men handing out the flyers were besieged by outstretched hands until all their flyers were gone. Copies were brought to Paul, who stared momentarily at the flyer in silence. He rushed outside to find the two men.

"Where did you get these from? Who gave you these?"

"A young lawyer pay me two hundred dollars to hand out these. He say he work for -"

"Hugh Turner, of course," said Paul, finishing his statement for him.

☙❧

Two days after the town hall meeting, The *Standard* ran an article by Sheri Gooding headlined, *Foreign land ownership legislation coming.*

The bloggers and social networkers immediately pounced on land ownership legislation, referring to it as LOL.

The article quoted an unnamed source as confirming that government was drafting legislation to restrict the purchase of land in Barbados by non-nationals. The story was confirmed the following day by the Prime Minister, who repeated that details on the content of the legislation had not yet been finalized but it would be coming soon.

An angry real estate community was well represented on the call-in programmes and the letter columns of the press. Property purchased by foreigners represented a large part of the total business of the bigger agencies. They felt that this was a predictable backlash to the Bathsheba situation and blamed the developer.

Paul Kyaki and the opponents of the Bathsheba development called the planned legislation a victory for the people. "When the people lead, the government has no choice but to follow," Paul proclaimed.

The residents on the hill in Bathsheba were angry. They felt that something had been taken away from them by people who put their personal politics above the interests of people less fortunate than they.

"What difference could it make to Barbados if the thirteen of us owners of the land on the hill were allowed to sell our properties?" asked Rabbit.

The letters arrived by motorcycle courier one afternoon, informing the landowners that the offers were still on the table but because of impending legislation they now had a deadline to confirm their willingness to sell their property. Monica Devonish had not yet received a letter but found out when Rabbit brought his to her. She called Tony. "We won the war but I am afraid we lost the battle."

Sheri Gooding did the story on this latest development and the opponents of the project reacted with anger.

"I-Sher, there is a man on the phone who wants to speak to you and you only. He refuses to give his name," said the telephone operator to Sheri on the morning the latest story appeared.

"Put him on," she said.

"The man behind the Bathsheba development is David King. He lives in St. James at a house called Ping Wing." The caller gave her a phone number and hung up without even saying goodbye. Sheri recognized the flat, rhythmic tone of voice as that of a real estate agent she had spoken to previously. She did a Doodle search for David King then picked up the phone and called Ping Wing.

"Mr. King is not here at the moment. Would you like to leave a message?"

Sheri did not leave a message.

She sat back in her chair, tapping the rubber end of a pencil on the pad in front of her and nibbling at her bottom lip. She reached for the phone.

"Mr. Turner, thank you for taking my call. I am doing a story on David King, the man behind the Bathsheba development. You have known Mr. King for a long time. What is his motivation for wanting to do this particular project?"

"Hold on a minute. Who told you Mr. King is the person doing this development?"

"I just got off the phone from Ping Wing. Are you denying that David King is the developer?"

"I am not denying or confirming anything."

"Thank you, Mr. Turner"

"Wait, hold on. What are you thanking me for? I haven't told you anything"

"Yes, you did, sir."

Sheri hung up, turned off her tape recorder and, fingers flying, she launched into an attack on her computer keyboard. Turner's refusal to deny was a good enough confirmation of her anonymous caller's allegation.

Hugh Turner was annoyed with himself. He felt he had permitted the confidence of the reporter, the speed of the conversation and the simple but classic lawyer's and journalist's question "Do you deny?" to trip him up. He called David King on his cellular phone.

The *Standard* ran the story the next day under the headline:

The man behind the Bathsheba development.

"The attorney for the controversial Bathsheba development project refused yesterday evening to deny that David King, the charismatic British multi-millionaire property developer, is the man behind the project," the article began. It went on to provide some biographical details on Mr. King, including that he maintained residences in Spain, Morocco, Switzerland, and Barbados, where he had been involved in two major real estate developments. "One of those developments, a block of condos nicknamed *King's Kong* by locals because of its overly imposing frontage, had remained empty after completion, victim of the recession but also of its controversial appearance."

"King was born in the East end of London to a single mother, left school at fifteen and first worked in the markets before entering the building trade, eventually becoming a very successful contractor then property developer. He has been twice married and divorced and is the father of two sons and a daughter. He is a keen football fan and a supporter of West Ham. He is known to give generously to charities." The story was accompanied by a photo of David King at a local fundraising event.

ન્જ્જ

The British press sent journalists to report on the story. One UK publication disclosed that the project was to be called "New Sybaris."

David King hopped on a chartered yacht and sailed down to the Grenadines. Phyllis Gertler flew from Zurich to join him there.

Sooner than was expected the government announced that it was ready to bring the "Alien Landholdings Act" to Parliament. The bloggers and social networkers called it *ALA*. Under the act, non-Barbadians would only be able to purchase property in designated areas or from other non-Barbadians. This had an immediate calming effect on the rhetoric. Once again the people on the hill in Bathsheba saw the game swinging away from them.

"You are not going to believe this," Sheri shouted down the telephone to a sleepy Tony Holford. "I have just finished reading the proposed legislation. The restriction on foreign ownership does not take effect until one year after its passage. They are giving these people a year's notice. Why the hell would they do that?"

"Shit, I don't know. Just when we thought this was over. I'll ask Monica tomorrow."

"I'll call her now. It's only 10:30, she is probably still up."

The *Standard* ran Sheri's article the following day quoting an unnamed attorney who thought that the delayed effective date of the sale of land by Bajans to foreigners was to permit existing contracts to be completed without prejudice. This meant that the way was clear for New Sybaris.

"Mr. Moderator, I wish to warn the people of the hill in Bathsheba to beware of the Greeks even when they bring gifts. This New Sybaris is nothing but a Trojan Horse," said one regular caller to a popular call-in programme.

"Mr. Moderator, you mean we have to put cricket in everything? This thing to do with the foreigners buying up all the land 'bout here keep swinging one way and then the next. This is like the game of glorious uncertainties," said another regular caller.

The deferred date meant that the deal on the hill was still alive and there was still considerable opposition to this outside of Bathsheba. But it was becoming muted as some opponents seemed willing to accept this as a last deal and even wished the residents there well.

The Aliens Landholdings Act was passed with the full consent of Parliament, including the MP for Bathsheba. He explained to his constituents that the one year delay was his idea and his way of protecting their opportunity.

A week later, a sombre-faced, unshaven David King sat in his office in his Spanish villa. He picked up a letter-sized brown envelope, stared once more at the sender's address in the UK, his original home address under a false name. He inserted the envelope into the shredder next to his desk. He listened to the whir of the machine while he looked out over the pool at the landscaped grounds. When the shredder stopped he turned his attention to the laptop on his desk. After a quick reread of the message on the screen, he hit send. It was an email to Hugh Turner instructing him to discontinue all action related to the purchase of properties on the hill and to issue the following press release.

"It is with much regret that Sybaris Properties (Barbados) Inc. announces the cessation of its plans in relation to the Bathsheba development. When this project was conceived, it never occurred to the developers that it would cause any controversy whatsoever. We sincerely believed that we were doing something for the benefit of the people of Bathsheba and Barbados, a country that our chairman holds in the highest affection. We sincerely apologise for any offense which we may have caused and wish the good people of Barbados the very best for the future."

The news was received with great bitterness by the people on the hill and many in the wider Bathsheba community. Lawyers poured over the correspondence between Prudence Chambers and the residents, looking for any possibility of breach of contract, but Hugh Turner had included a couple of preconditions to completion of agreement that made lawsuits out of the question.

There was widespread speculation on the real reason King withdrew. In this land of rumours there were many stories, so many stories that knowing which ones to believe was a mark of one's intimacy with the cultural landscape of this small complex island. One story alleged that he had been threatened with exposure for tax evasion back in England. Another said that he had been offered a better alternative deal. But the story most frequently whispered said that King had been sent a set of compromising photos of himself in a Bangkok hotel room with an under-aged prostitute, along with an accompanying note asking him to please call off the Bathsheba project, or so the story went.

Paul Kyaki and his supporters celebrated. As a guest on a call-in programme, he used the opportunity to inform the public that he intended to start a new, as yet unnamed political party. One caller, a man with a very deep voice, after congratulating Paul on his decision, suggested that the new party should be called the Party of Oppressed Peoples. "That's not a bad suggestion but I am sure we will have others," responded Paul to rising snickers and outright laughter from the production crew. A crew member said the word, "Acronym." Paul rounded on the caller with an expletive-laden outburst, half of which was heard by the listeners as the distracted crew was slow to cut off the broadcast. The newspapers reported on the incident and several readers responded by offering other suggestions, all with amusing acronyms, for the name of the party.

❧❦

There were no celebrations in Bathsheba. Bathsheba was devastated; some villagers no longer spoke to those who had come down on the opposite side to them. Of the people on the hill, only Rabbit spoke to Tony.

Life was settling down, but people were still quarrelling.

❧❦

There was a loud bang immediately followed by the whoosh of a muffled explosion as the Molotov cocktail smashed against the purpleheart wood outside of Tony's bedroom. The sound jolted him upright and the sight of flames flashing through his bedroom window propelled him off the bed. His hand knocked over the empty rum bottle by the side of the bed as he fell to the floor.

He picked himself up and ran outside in his underwear, grabbed his garden hose and fumbled to attach it to the tap.

He raced around to the fire. He was joined by Tyrone, his next door neighbour, his hose in hand. Together they managed to put out the fire.

The hardwood had been slow to ignite and had bought them valuable time.

ॐ✖

Speculation about the possible motives of David King continued to occupy the attention of the press and radio for some time after the fall of New Sybaris.

David did get to meet the Prime Minister after all. It was at a charity event. He walked over to the Prime Minister and introduced himself.

David offered his congratulations on the passing of the Alien Landholdings Act. "The Government of Barbados did the right thing for all concerned," he said. "When I was a boy, I used to go with my grandmother to the markets in the East End of London. Whenever an item was in short supply, the price increased. I learned a valuable lesson then. If you limit a commodity you increase its value, the more limited, the more valuable."

The Prime Minister's smile disappeared. "What do you mean? Your offer to those people in Bathsheba was some sort of a gambit?"

"Oh, no, my offer was sincere."

"Really? You know, your lawyer told me that you never lose. Perhaps he meant you never admit when you have lost."

King smiled, "Wait and see what happens to the value of foreign owned property in Barbados Mr. Prime Minister. Wait and see."

A year later real estate values of foreign-owned properties in Barbados had added back all the value they lost during the recession years and continued their upward rise. King and partners sold *King's Kong* for an undisclosed sum, rumoured to be the highest price ever paid, per unit, for a condominium in Barbados.

ॐ✖

Tony was the last to arrive at the Waterfront Café in Bridgetown. He and Sheri had been invited by Monica and Peter for a celebratory drink. They couldn't do this in Bathsheba. He joined them at a round table on the outside next to the careenage.

"What do you want to drink, Tony?" asked Peter.

"I'll have a Mount Gay Black with a little water," Tony said without hesitation. Peter raised his hand and a waitress came over. Tony settled into a metal chair facing north across the water. Behind him, from the inside of the café, a jazzman's horn wailed. In front of him the fishing boats and yachts bounced and swayed gently in the water, masts and antennae twisted and rocked slowly from side to side like languid windshield wipers. Through these he could see Heroes Square with its solitary statue of Lord Horatio Nelson and beyond the square the classic colonial architecture of the parliament buildings, now dwarfed by the naked concrete cylinders of the modern Central Bank of Barbados building in the background. He stopped his mind mid-thought on the complexities of modern Barbados. He frowned then turned his gaze to his companions and smiled that shy smile of his.

The End

20257748R00083

Made in the USA
Charleston, SC
03 July 2013